"I've Been Thinking About That Kiss."

Oh, he'd been thinking about it, too. About what he would have done if they'd been alone in the dark.

Garrett looked at her and knew instantly thinking about it had been a mistake. Desire glittered in her eyes. He recognized it, because the same thing was happening to him. He couldn't seem to fight it. More, he didn't want to.

He hadn't asked for this. Didn't need it. But the truth was, he wanted Alexis.

The worst part? He couldn't have her.

He was working for her father. She was a princess. He was responsible for her safety. In the real world, a holiday romance was right up his alley. No strings. No complications. But *this* woman was nothing *but* complications.

Good reasons for avoiding this situation, he told himself. For keeping an eye on her from a distance.

And not one of those reasons meant a damn thing in the face of the need clawing his insides.

* * *

Dear Reader,

I *love* old movies. From romantic comedies to thrillers to ghost stories. The old movies—and I'm talking really old movies from the forties and fifties—all had a kind of magic you don't see very often today.

And one of my absolute favorites has always been *Roman Holiday,* the story of a princess who runs away from her royal duties for a day of freedom.

In *To Kiss a King,* I was able to change that idea up a little and give it the romantic happily ever after it deserved. My royal princess, Alexis, escapes palace life to experience real life. And she starts out with her dream trip to Disneyland. Which, of course, since it's my book, is where she meets Garrett King.

Garrett's a security expert, and when he discovers that Alex is a runaway princess, he's torn between protecting her and seducing her.

And that, I think, makes for a whirlwind romance filled with secrets, lies, seduction and—I sincerely hope—a wonderful love story.

I hope you enjoy *To Kiss a King* and I'd love to hear from you! Find me on Facebook or Twitter and email me at maureenchildbooks@gmail.com.

Happy reading!

Maureen

MAUREEN CHILD

TO KISS A KING

Harlequin Desire

Recycling programs
for this product may
not exist in your area.

ISBN-13: 978-0-373-73150-3

TO KISS A KING

Copyright © 2012 by Maureen Child

This edition published by arrangement with Harlequin Books S.A.

For questions and comments about the quality of this book please contact us
at Customer_eCare@Harlequin.ca.

® and TM are trademarks of Harlequin Books S.A., used under license.
Trademarks indicated with ® are registered in the United States Patent
and Trademark Office, the Canadian Trade Marks Office and in other
countries.

www.Harlequin.com

Printed in U.S.A.

MAUREEN CHILD

is a California native who loves to travel. Every chance they get, she and her husband are taking off on another research trip. The author of more than sixty books, Maureen loves a happy ending and still swears that she has the best job in the world. She lives in Southern California with her husband, two children and a golden retriever with delusions of grandeur. Visit Maureen's website, www.maureenchild.com.

To Susan Mallery, a great writer and an
even better friend. For all of the shared dreams,
all of the good laughs and all those yet to come.
Thanks, Susan.

One

Garrett King was in Hell.

Dozens of screaming, laughing children raced past him and he winced as their voices hit decibels only dogs should have been able to hear. Happiest Place on Earth? He didn't think so.

How he had let himself be talked into this, he had no idea.

"Getting soft," he muttered darkly and leaned one hand on the hot metal balustrade in front of him only to wrench his hand back instantly. He glanced at his palm, sighed and reached for a napkin out of his cousin's bag to wipe the sticky cotton candy off his skin.

"You could be at the office," he told himself sternly, wadding up the napkin and tossing it into a trash can. "You could be checking invoices, keeping tabs on the new client. But no, you had to say yes to your cousin instead."

Jackson King had pulled out all the stops getting Garrett to go along with this little family adventure. Jackson's wife, Casey, was apparently "worried" because Garrett was alone too much. Nice woman Casey, he told himself. But did no one ever consider that maybe a man was alone because he *wanted* to be?

But he still could have begged off if it had been just Casey and Jackson doing the asking. But Garrett's cousin had cheated.

He had had his daughters ask "Uncle" Garrett to go with them and frankly, when faced with three of the cutest kids in the world, it would have been impossible to say no. And Jackson knew it, the clever bastard.

"Hey, cuz!" Jackson's shout sounded out and Garrett turned to give him a hard look.

Jackson only laughed. "Casey, honey," he said, turning to his stunning wife, "did you see that? I don't think Garrett's having any fun."

"About that," Garrett cut in, lifting his voice to be heard over the raucous noise rising from the crowd, "I was thinking I'd just head out now. Leave you guys to some family fun."

"You *are* family, Garrett," Casey pointed out.

Before he could speak, Garrett felt a tug at his pants leg. He looked down into Mia's upturned face. "Uncle Garrett, we're going on the fast mountain ride. You wanna come?"

At five, Mia King was already a heartbreaker. From her King blue eyes to the missing front tooth to the dimple in her cheek, she was absolutely adorable. And not being a dummy, she knew how to work it already, too.

"Uh…" Garrett glanced behind Mia to her younger sisters Molly and Mara. Molly was three and Mara was just beginning to toddle. The three of them were unstoppable, Garrett told himself wryly.

There was just no way he was getting out of this day

early. One girl pouting was hard to resist. Three were too much for any man to stand against.

"How about I stand here and watch your stuff while you guys go on the ride?"

Jackson snorted a laugh that Garrett ignored. For God's sake, he owned the most respected security company in the country and here he was haggling with a five-year-old.

Garrett and Jackson had been good friends for years. Most of the King cousins were close, but he and Jackson had worked closely together over the years. Garrett's security company and Jackson's company, King Jets, fed off each other. With Garrett's high-priced clients renting Jackson's luxury jets, both companies were thriving for the loosely defined partnership.

Jackson's wife, Casey, on the other hand, was one of those happily married women who saw every determined bachelor as a personal challenge.

"You going on the Matterhorn with us?" Jackson asked, plucking Mara from his wife's arms. The chubby toddler slapped at his cheeks gleefully and Garrett watched with some amusement as Jackson practically melted. The man was a sap when it came to his family. Funny, because in business, Jackson King was a cutthroat kind of guy that nobody wanted to cross.

"Nope," Garrett told him and lifted the baby out of his cousin's arms. With the crazed population explosion in the King family, Garrett was getting used to dealing with kids. Comfortably settling the tiny girl on his hip, he said, "I'll wait here with Mara and the rest of your—" he paused to glance down at the stroller and the bags already piled high on it "—stuff."

"You could ride with me," Mia insisted, turning those big blue eyes on him.

"Oh, she's good," Jackson whispered on a laugh.

Garrett went down on one knee and looked her in the eye. "How about I stay here with your sister and you tell me all about the ride when you get off?"

She scowled a little, clearly unused to losing, then grinned. "Okay."

Casey took both of the girls' hands, smiled at Garrett and headed for the line.

"I didn't ask you to come along so you could just stand around, you know," Jackson said.

"Yeah. Why did you ask me along? Better yet, why'd I say yes?"

Jackson laughed, looked over his shoulder at his wife and then said, "One word. Casey. She thinks you're lonely. And if you think I'm going to listen to her worry about you all by myself, you're nuts."

Mara slapped Garrett's face. He swiveled his head to smile at the baby. "Your daddy's scared of your mommy."

"Damn straight," Jackson admitted with a laugh. He headed off after the rest of his family and called back, "If she gets cranky, there's a bottle in the diaper bag."

"I think I can handle a baby," he shouted back, but Jackson was already swallowed by the crowd.

"It's just you and me, kid," Garrett told the girl who laughed delightedly and squirmed as if she wanted to be turned loose to run. "Oh, no, you don't. I put you down, you disappear and your mommy kills me."

"Down." Mara looked mutinous.

"No."

She scowled again then tried a coy smile.

"Man," Garrett said with a smile. "Are women *born* knowing how to do that?"

Bright, cheerful calliope music erupted from somewhere nearby and the smell of popcorn floated on the breeze. A dog wearing a top hat was waltzing with Cinderella to the cheers of the crowd. And Garrett was holding a baby and feeling as out of place as—hell, he couldn't even think of anything as out of place as he felt at the moment.

This was not his world, he thought, jiggling Mara when she started fussing. Give Garrett King a dangerous situation, a shooter going after a high-profile target, a kidnapping, even a jewelry heist, and he was in his element.

This happy, shiny stuff? Not so much.

Owning and operating the biggest, most successful security company in the country was bound to color your outlook on the world. Their clients ranged from royalty to wealthy industrialists, computer billionaires and politicians. Because of their own immense wealth, the King brothers knew how to blend in when arranging security. Because of their expertise, their reputation kept growing. Their firm was the most sought-after of its kind on the planet. The King twins flew all over the world to meet the demands of their clients. And he and his twin, Griffin, were good with that. Not everyone could be relaxed and optimistic. There had to be people like he and Griff around to take care of the dirty jobs.

That was his comfort zone, he told himself as he watched Jackson and his family near the front of the line. Casey was holding Molly and Jackson had Mia up on his shoulders. They looked…perfect. And Garrett was glad for his cousin, really. In fact, he was happy for all of the Kings who had recently jumped off a cliff into the uncharted waters of marriage and family. But he wouldn't be joining them.

Guys like him didn't do happy endings.

"That's okay, though," he whispered, planting a kiss on Mara's forehead. "I'll settle for spending time with you guys. How's that?"

She burbled something he took as agreement then fixed her gaze on a bright pink balloon. "Boon!"

Garrett was just going to buy it for her when he noticed the woman.

Alexis Morgan Wells was having a *wonderful* day. Disneyland was everything she had hoped it would be. She loved everything about it. The music, the laughter. The cartoon characters wandering around interacting with the crowd. She loved the gardens, the topiary statues; she even loved the smell of the place. It was like childhood and dreams and magic all at once.

The music from the last ride she'd been on was still dancing through her mind—she had a feeling it would be for hours—when she noticed the man coming up to her. Her good mood quickly drained away as the same man who had followed her on to It's a Small World hurried to catch up. He'd had the seat behind her in the boat and had come close to ruining the whole experience for her as he insisted on trying to talk to her.

Just as he was now.

"Come on, babe. I'm not a crazy person or anything. I just want to buy you lunch. Is that so bad?"

She half turned and gave him a patient, if tight, smile. "I've already told you I'm not interested, so please go away."

Instead of being rebuffed, his eyes lit up. "You're British, aren't you? The accent's cool."

"Oh, for heaven's sake."

She was really going to have to work on that, she told herself sternly. If she wasn't paying close attention, her clipped accent immediately branded her as "different." Though it would take a much better ear than that of the man currently bothering her, to recognize that her accent wasn't British, but Cadrian.

But if she worked at it, she could manage an American accent—since her mother had been born in California. Thinking about her mom brought a quick zip of guilt shooting through her, but Alex tamped it down. She'd deal with it later. She was absolutely sure her mother would understand why Alex had had to leave—she was just in no hurry to hear how much worry she'd caused by taking off.

After all, Alex was a bright, capable adult and if she wanted a vacation, why should she have to jump through hoops to take one? There, she was feeling better already. Until she picked up on the fact that her would-be admirer was still talking. Honestly, she was trying to stay under the radar and this man was drawing way too much attention to her.

Trying to ignore him, Alex quickened her steps, moving in and out of the ever-shifting crowd with the grace earned from years of dance lessons. She wore a long, tunic-style white blouse, blue jeans and blue platform heels, and, at the moment, she was wishing she'd worn sneakers. Then she could have sprinted for some distance.

The minute that thought entered her mind, she dismissed it, though. Running through a crowd like a lunatic would only draw the notice she was trying to avoid.

"C'mon, babe, it's *lunch*. What could it hurt?"

"I don't eat," she told him, "I'm an oxygenarian."

He blinked at her. "What?"

"Nothing," she muttered, hurrying again. Stop talking to him, she told herself. Ignore him and he'll go away.

She headed for the landmark right ahead of her. The snow-topped mountain in the middle of Anaheim, California. This particular mountain was probably one of the best known peaks in the world. Alex smiled just looking at it. She lifted her gaze and watched as toboggans filled with screaming, laughing people jolted around curves and splashed through lagoons, sending waves of water into the air. The line for the mountain was a long one and as her gaze moved over the people there, she saw *him*. He was watching her. A big man with black hair, a stern jaw and a plump baby on his hip.

In one quick instant, she felt a jolt of something like "recognition." As if something inside her, *knew* him. Had been searching for him. Unfortunately, judging by the black-haired little girl he was holding, some other woman had found him first.

"Quit walking so fast, will ya?" the annoying guy behind her whined.

Alex fixed her gaze on the sharp-eyed man and felt his stare hit her as powerfully as a touch. Then his eyes shifted from her to the man behind her and back again. He seemed to understand the situation instantly.

"There you are, honey!" he called out, smiling directly at Alex. "What took you so long?"

Smiling broadly, she accepted the help he was offering and ran to him. He greeted her with a grin then dropped one arm around her shoulders, pulling her in close to his side. Only then did he shift his gaze to the disappointed man.

"There a problem here?" Her Knight in Shining Denim demanded.

"No," the guy muttered, shaking his head. "No problem. Later."

And he was gone.

Alex watched him go with a sigh of relief. Not that he had ever scared her or anything, but she hadn't wanted to waste her first day in Disneyland being irritated. The big man beside her still had his arm around her and Alex liked it. He was big and strong and it was hard not to appreciate a guy who had seen you needed help and offered it without a qualm.

"Boon!"

The little girl's voice shattered the moment and with that reminder that her hero was probably someone else's husband, Alex slipped out from under his arm. Glancing up at the little girl, she smiled. "You're a beauty, aren't you? Your daddy must be very proud."

"Oh, he is," the man beside her said, his voice so deep it seemed to sink right inside her. "And he's got two more just like her."

"Really." She wasn't sure why the news that he was the father of three was so disappointing, but there it was.

"Yeah. My cousin and his wife have the other two on the ride right now. I'm just watching this one for them."

"Oh." She smiled, pleasure rushing through her. "Then you're not her father?"

He smiled, too, as if he knew exactly what she was thinking. "Not a chance. I wouldn't do that to some poor, unsuspecting kid."

Alex looked into his eyes and enjoyed the sparkle she found there. He was relishing this little flirtation as much as she was. "Oh, I don't know. A hero might make a very good father."

"Hero? I'm hardly that."

"You were for me a minute ago," she said. "I couldn't seem to convince that man to leave me alone, so I really appreciate your help."

"You're welcome. But you could have gone to a security guard and had the guy thrown out. Probably should have."

No, going to a security guard would have involved making statements, filling out paperwork and then her identity would be revealed and the lovely day she'd planned would have been ruined.

She shook her head, pushed her long blond hair back from her face and turned to sweep her gaze across the manicured flower gardens, the happy kids and the brilliant blue sky overhead. "No, he wasn't dangerous. Just irritating."

He laughed and she liked the sound of it.

"Boon, Gar," the little girl said in a voice filled with the kind of determination only a single-minded toddler could manage.

"Right. Balloon." He lifted one hand to the balloon seller, and the guy stepped right up, gently tying the string of a bright pink balloon to the baby's wrist. While Garrett paid the man, the baby waved her arm, squealing with delight as the balloon danced and jumped to her whim.

"So, I think introductions are in order," he said. "This demanding female is Mara and I'm Garrett."

"Alexis, but call me Alex," she said, holding her right hand out to him.

He took her hand in his and the instant her skin brushed along his, Alex felt ripples of something really intriguing washing throughout her body. Then he let her go and the delightful heat dissipated.

"So, Alex, how's your day going?"

She laughed a little. "Until that one little moment, it was going great. I love it here. It's my first time, and I've heard so much about this place…"

"Ah," he said nodding, "that explains it."

She tensed. "Explains what?"

"If it's your first time here, you're having so much fun that all of these crowds don't bother you."

"Oh, no. I think it's wonderful. Everyone seems so nice, well, except for—"

"That one little moment?" he asked, repeating her words to her.

"Yes, exactly." Alex smiled again and reluctantly took a step back. As lovely as this was, talking to a handsome man who had no idea who she was, it would be better for her if she ended it now and went on her way. "Thank you again for the rescue, but I should really be going…"

He tipped his head to one side and looked at her. "Meeting someone?"

"No, but—"

"Then what's your hurry?"

Her heartbeat sped up at the invitation in his eyes. He didn't want her to leave. And how nice that was. He actually liked her.

The darling little girl was still playing with her balloon, paying no attention at all to the two adults with her.

Alex looked up into Garrett's pale blue eyes and did some fast thinking. She had to keep a low profile, true. But that didn't mean she had to be a hermit during her… vacation, did it? And what kind of holiday would it be if there were no "romance" included?

"What do you say," he added, "hang with us today. Rescue me from a day filled with too many kids?"

"*You* need rescuing?"

She saw the teasing glint in his eyes and responded to it with a smile.

"Trust me. My cousin's girls all have my number. If you're not there to protect me, who knows what might happen?"

Tempting, she thought. So very tempting. She'd only been in America for three days and already she was feeling a little isolated. Being on her own was liberating, but, as it turned out, *lonely*. And it wasn't as if she could call the few friends she had in the States—the moment she did, word would get back to her family and, just like that, her bid for freedom would end.

What could it hurt to spend the day with a man who made her toes curl and the family he clearly loved? She took a breath and made the leap. "All right, thank you. I would love to rescue you."

"Excellent. My cousin and his family should be back any minute now. So while we wait, why don't you tell me where you're from. I can't quite place your accent. It's British, but…not."

She jolted a little and fought to keep him from seeing it. "You've a good ear."

"So I've been told. But that's not really an answer, is it?"

No, it wasn't, and how astute of him to notice. She'd been trained in how to answer questions without really answering them from the time she was a child. Her father would have been proud. *Never answer a question directly, Alexis. Always be vague. Watch what you say, Alexis. You've a responsibility to your family. Your heritage. Your people…*

"Hey. Alex."

At the sound of his concerned voice, she shook her head, coming out of her thoughts with relief. That was the second time Garrett had rescued her today. She didn't want to think about her duties. Her role in history. She didn't want to be anything but Alex.

So instead of being evasive again, she said, "Why don't you try to figure out where I'm from and I'll let you know when you've got it right?"

One dark eyebrow lifted. "Oh, you're challenging the wrong guy. But you're on. Five bucks says I've got it by the end of the day."

Oh, she hoped not. If he did, that would ruin everything. But she braved it out and asked, "Five dollars? Not much of a wager."

He gave her a slow grin that sent new flashes of heat dancing through her system. "I'm open to negotiation."

She actually *felt* her blood sizzle and hum.

"No, no. That's all right." She backed up quickly. Maybe she wasn't as prepared for that zing of romance as she had thought. Or maybe Garrett the Gorgeous was just too much for her to handle. Either way, she was nervous enough to try to cool things down between them just a little. "Five dollars will do. It's a bargain."

"Agreed," he said, one corner of his mouth lifting tantalizingly. "But just so you know, you should never bet with me, Alex. I always win."

"Confident, aren't you?"

"You have no idea."

A thrill of something hot and delicious swept through her veins. Nerves or not, she really enjoyed what he was doing to her. What was it about him that affected her so?

"That was fun, Uncle Garrett!"

A tiny whirlwind rushed up to them and threw both arms around Garrett's knees. The girl gave him a wide smile then shifted suspicious eyes to Alex. "Who are you?"

"This is Alex," Garrett told her. "Alex, meet Mia."

She smiled at the child and couldn't help noticing that the little girl held on to Garrett's legs just a little more tightly.

"Mia, don't run from me in these crowds," a deep male voice shouted.

Alex turned to watch an impossibly attractive couple approach, the man holding on to a smaller version of the still-wary Mia.

"Alex," Garrett said briskly, "this is my cousin Jackson and his wife, Casey, and that pretty girl with them is Molly."

"It's lovely to meet you all."

Jackson gave her a quick up and down, then winked at his wife. "Wow, leave Garrett alone for a few minutes and he finds the most beautiful woman in the whole place—"

His wife nudged him with an elbow.

"—not counting you of course, sweetie. You're the most beautiful woman in the *world*."

"Nice recovery," Casey told him with a laugh and a smile for Alex.

"Always were a smooth one, Jackson," Garrett mused.

"It's why she loves me," his cousin answered, dropping a kiss on his wife's head.

Alex smiled at all of them. It was lovely to see the open affection in this family, though she felt a sharp pang of envy slice at her, as well. To get some time for herself she'd had to run from her own family. She missed them, even her dictatorial father, and being around these people only brought up their loss more sharply.

"It's nice to meet you, Alex," Casey said, extending her right hand in welcome.

"Thank you. I must admit I'm a little overwhelmed by everything. This is my first trip to Disneyland and—"

"Your *first* time?" Mia interrupted. "But you're *old*."

"Mia!" Casey was horrified.

Garrett and Jackson laughed and Alex joined them. Bending down slightly, she met Mia's gaze and said, "It's horrible I know. But I live very far away from here, so this is the first chance I've ever had to visit."

"Oh." Nodding her head, Mia thought about it for a minute then looked at her mother. "I think we should take Alex to the ghost ride."

"Mia, that's *your* favorite ride," her father said.

"But she would like it, wouldn't you, Alex?" She turned her eyes up and gave her a pleading look.

"You know," Alex said, "I was just wishing I knew how to find the ghost ride."

"I'll show you!" Mia took her hand and started walking, fully expecting her family to follow.

"Guess you'll be spending the day with us for sure, now," Garrett teased.

"Looks that way." She grinned, delighted with this turn of events. She was in a place she'd heard about her whole life and she wasn't alone. There were children to enjoy and people to talk to and it was very near to perfect.

Then she looked up at Garrett's blue eyes and told herself maybe it was closer to perfect than she knew.

"And after the ghost ride, we can ride the jungle boats and then the pirate one." Mia was talking a mile a minute.

"Molly, honey, don't pick up the bug," Jackson said patiently.

"Bug?" Casey repeated, horrified.

Still holding Mara, Garrett came up beside Alex and said softly, "I promise, after the ghost ride, I'll ride herd on my family and you can do what you want to do."

The funny thing was, he didn't know it, but she was already doing what she had always wanted to do.

She *wanted* to be accepted. To spend a day with nothing more to worry about than enjoying herself. And mostly, she wanted to meet people and have them like her because she was Alex Wells.

Not because she was Her Royal Highness Princess Alexis Morgan Wells of Cadria.

Two

She was driving Garrett just a little crazy.

And not only because she was beautiful and funny and smart. But because he'd never seen a woman let go and really enjoy herself so much. Most of the women who came and went from his life were more interested in how their hair looked. Or in being sophisticated enough that a ride on spinning teacups would never have entered their heads.

But Alex was different. She had the girls eating out of her hand, and, without even trying, she was reaching Garrett in ways that he never would have expected. He couldn't take his eyes off her.

That wide smile was inviting, sexy—and familiar, somehow.

He knew he'd seen her before somewhere, but damned if he could remember where. And that bothered him, too. Because a woman like Alex wasn't easily forgotten.

At lunch, she had bitten into a burger with a sigh of pleasure so rich that all he could think of was cool sheets and hot sex. She sat astride a carousel horse and he imagined her straddling him. She licked at an ice cream cone and he—

Garrett shook his head and mentally pulled back fast from that particular image. As it was, he was having a hard time walking. A few more thoughts like that one and he'd be paralyzed.

Alex loved everything about Disneyland. He saw it in her eyes because she didn't hide a thing. Another way she was different from the women he knew. They were all about artful lies, strategic moves and studied flirtation.

Alex was just…herself.

"You'll like this, Alex," said Mia, who had appointed herself Alex's personal tour guide. "The pirate ships shoot cannons and there's a fire and singing, too. And it's dark inside."

"Okay, kiddo," Jackson told his daughter, interrupting her flood of information, "how about we give Alex a little rest?" He grinned at her and Garrett as he steered his family into the front row of the boat.

Garrett took the hint gratefully and pulled Alexis into the last row. A bit of separation for the duration of the ride would give them a little time to themselves.

"She's wonderful," Alex murmured. "So bright. So talkative."

"Oh, she is that," Garrett said with a laugh. "Mia has an opinion on everything and doesn't hesitate to share it. Her kindergarten teacher calls her 'precocious.' I call her a busybody."

She laughed again and Garrett found himself smiling in response. There was no cautious titter. No careful chuckle. When Alex laughed, she threw her soul into it and everything about her lit up. Oh, he was getting in way too deep. This was ridiculous. Not only did he not even know her last name, but he hadn't been able to pin down what country she was from, either.

Not for lack of trying, though.

The sense of familiarity he had for her was irritating as hell. There was something there. Something just out of reach, that would tell him how he knew her. Who she was. And yet, he couldn't quite grab hold of it.

The ride jolted into motion and Alex leaned forward, eager to see everything. He liked that about her, too. Her curiosity. Her appreciation for whatever was happening. It wasn't something enough people did, living in the moment. For most, it was all about "tomorrow." What they would do when they had the time or the money or the energy.

He'd seen it all too often. People who had everything in the world and didn't seem to notice because they were always looking forward to the next thing.

"Wonderful," she whispered. Their boat rocked lazily on its tracks, water slapping at its hull. She looked behind them at the people awaiting the next boat then shifted her gaze to his.

Overhead, a night sky was filled with stars and animatronic fireflies blinked on and off. A sultry, hot breeze wafted past them. Even in the darkness, he saw delight shining in her eyes and the curve of her mouth was something he just didn't want to resist any longer.

Leaning forward, he caught her by the back of the neck and pulled her toward him. Then he slanted his mouth over hers for a taste of the mouth that had been driving him nuts for hours.

She was worth the wait.

After a second's surprise, she recovered and kissed him

back. Her mouth moved against his with a soft, languid touch that stirred fires back into life and made him wish they were all alone in the dark—rather than surrounded by singing pirates and chattering tourists.

She sighed and leaned into him and that fired him up so fast, it took his breath away. But who needed breathing anyway? She lifted one hand to his cheek and when she pulled back, breaking the kiss, her fingertips stroked his jaw. She drew a breath and let it go again with a smile. Leaning into him, she whispered, "That was lovely."

He took her hand in his and kissed the center of her palm. "It was way better than lovely."

A kid squealed, a pirate's gun erupted too close to the boat and Alex jolted in surprise. Then she laughed with delight and eased back against him, pillowing her head on his shoulder. He pulled her in more closely to him and, instead of watching the ride, indulged himself by watching her reactions to their surroundings instead.

Her eyes never stopped shifting. Her smile never faltered. She took it all in, as if she were soaking up experiences like a sponge. And in that moment, Garrett was pitifully glad Jackson had talked him into going to Disneyland.

"I'm having such a nice day," she whispered in a voice pitched low enough that Garrett almost missed it.

"*Nice?* That's it?"

She tipped her head back and smiled up at him. "*Very* nice."

"Oh, well then, that's better." He snorted and shook his head. Nothing a man liked better than hearing the woman he was fantasizing about telling him she was having a "nice" time.

"Oh, look! The dog has the jail cell keys!" She was off again, losing herself in the moment and Garrett was charmed. The pirates were singing, water lapped at the sides of their boat and up ahead of them he could hear Mia singing along. He smiled to himself and realized that astonishing as it was, he, too, was having a *very* nice day.

After the ride, they walked into twilight. Sunset stained the sky with the last shreds of color before night crept in. The girls were worn-out. Molly was dragging, Mara was asleep on Casey's shoulder and Mia was so far beyond tired, her smile was fixed more in a grimace. But before they could go home, they had to make their traditional last stop.

"You'll like the castle, Alex," Mia said through a yawn. "Me and Molly are gonna be princesses someday and we're gonna have a castle like this one and we'll have puppies, too…"

"Again with the dog," Jackson said with a sigh at what was apparently a very familiar topic.

Alex chuckled and slipped her hand into Garrett's. His fingers closed over hers as he cut a glance her way. In the soft light, her eyes shone with the same excitement he'd seen earlier. She wasn't tired out by all the kids and the crowds. She was thriving on this.

Her mouth curved slightly and another ping of recognition hit him. Frowning to himself, Garrett tried to pin down where he'd seen her before. He knew he'd never actually *met* her before today. He wouldn't have forgotten that. But she was so damned familiar…

The castle shone with a pink tinge and as they approached, lights carefully hidden behind rocks and in the shrubbery blinked on to make it seem even more of a fairy-tale palace.

Garrett shook his head and smiled as Mia cooed in delight. Swans were floating gracefully in the lake. A cool wind rustled the trees and lifted the scent of the neatly trimmed rosebushes into the air.

"Can I have a princess hat?" Mia asked.

"Sure you can, sweetie," Jackson said, scooping his oldest into his arms for a fast hug.

Garrett watched the byplay and, for the first time, felt a twinge of regret. Not that it would last long, but for the moment, he could admit that the thought of having kids like Mia and her sisters wasn't an entirely hideous idea. For other people, of course. Not for him.

"Alex, look!" Mia grabbed Alex's hand and half dragged her up to the stone balustrade overlooking the lake. The two of them stood together, watching the swans, the pink castle in the background and Garrett stopped dead. And stared.

In one blinding instant, he knew why she looked so familiar.

Several years ago, he'd done some work for her father.

Her father, the King of Cadria.

Which meant that Alex the delicious, Alex the sexiest woman he'd ever known, was actually the Crown Princess Alexis.

And he'd kissed her.

Damn.

He scrubbed one hand across the back of his neck, took a deep breath and held it. This changed things. Radically.

"Do you want to live in a castle, Alex?" Mia asked.

Garrett listened for her answer.

Alex ran one hand over Mia's long black hair and said, "I think a castle might get lonely. They're awfully big, you know. And drafty, as well."

Garrett watched her face as she described what he knew was her home. Funny, he'd never imagined that a princess might not like her life. After all, in the grand scheme, being royalty had to be better than a lot of other alternatives.

"But I could have lots of puppies," Mia said thoughtfully.

"Yes, but you'd never see them because princesses can't play with puppies. They have more important things to do. They have to say all the right things, do all the right things. There's not a lot of time for playing."

Mia frowned at that.

So did Garrett. Was that how she really felt about her life? Was that why she was here, trying to be incognito? To escape her world? And what would she do if she knew he had figured out her real identity? Would she bolt?

Alex smiled and said, "I think you might not like a real castle as much as you do this one."

Nodding, the little girl murmured, "Maybe I'll just be a pretend princess."

"Excellent idea," Alex told her with another smile. Then she turned her head to look at Garrett and their gazes collided.

He felt the slam of attraction hit him like a fist to the chest. He was in deep trouble here. A princess, for God's sake? He'd kissed a *princess?* He took a good long look at her, from her platform heels to the blue jeans and the pair of sunglasses perched on top of her head.

She had worked very hard to disguise herself, he thought, and wondered why. As a princess, she could have had a guided tour through the park, swept through all of the lines and been treated like—well, royalty. Instead, she had spent her day wandering through Disneyland just like any other tourist.

Alone.

That word shouted through his mind and instantly, his professional side sat up and took notice. Letting go, for the moment, of the fact that she'd lied about who she was—where was her security detail? Where were her bodyguards? The entourage? Didn't she know how dangerous it was for someone like her to be unprotected? The world was a dangerous place and helping out the wackos by giving them a clear shot at you didn't seem like a good plan to him.

So just what was she up to?

As if reading his troubled thoughts from the emotions in his eyes, Alex's smile faded slightly. Garrett noticed and immediately put his game face on. She was keeping her identity a secret for a reason. Until he found out what that was, he'd play along.

And until he knew everything that was happening, he'd make damn sure she was safe.

In the huge parking lot, they all said goodbye and Jackson and Casey herded their girls off toward their car. The parking lot lights above them flickered weirdly as tourists streamed past like zombies in search of the best way home.

Garrett turned to look at Alex again. "Where's your car?"

"Oh, I don't have one," she said quickly. "I never learned to drive, so I took a cab here from the hotel."

A cab, he thought grimly. On her own. She was asking for disaster. It was a freaking miracle she'd made it here without somebody recognizing her and tipping off the press. "Where are you staying?"

"In Huntington Beach."

Not too far, he thought, but far enough that he didn't want her repeating the "grab a cab" thing. His gaze scanning the crowded lot and the people passing by them, he said, "I'll give you a ride back to your hotel."

"Oh, you don't have to do that," she argued automatically.

He wondered if it was sheer politeness or a reaction to his change in attitude. The closeness, the heat that had been between them earlier and definitely cooled. But how could it not? She was a runaway princess, and he was the guy who knew better than to give in to his urges, now that he knew the truth.

She was a *princess* for God's sake. Didn't matter that his bank account was probably close to hers. There was wealth and then there was *royalty.* The two didn't necessarily mix.

"Yeah," he told her, "I really do."

"I can take care of myself," she said.

"I'm sure you can. But why wait for a cab when I'm here and ready?"

No way was he going to let her out of his sight until he knew she was safe. She was too high-profile. Princess Alexis's pretty face had adorned more magazine covers than he could count. Reporters and photographers usually followed after her like rats after the Pied Piper. Her luck was bound to run out soon and once it did, she'd have people crowding all around her. And not all of them would be trustworthy.

Nope. He'd be with her until he got her back to her hotel, at least. Then he'd figure out what to do next.

"Well, all right then," she said with a smile. "Thank you."

The traffic gods were smiling on them and it didn't take more than twenty minutes before he was steering his BMW up to the waterfront hotel. He left his keys with the valet, took Alex's arm and escorted her into the hotel. His gaze never quit moving, checking out the area, the people, the situation. The hotel lobby was elegant and mostly empty. Live trees stood in huge, terra cotta pots on the inside of the double doors. A marble floor gleamed under pearly lights and tasteful paintings hung on cream-colored walls.

A couple of desk clerks were busily inputting things into computers. A guest stood at the concierge, asking questions, and an elevator hushed open to allow an elderly couple to exit. It all looked fine to his studied eyes, but as he knew all too well, things could change in an instant. An ordinary moment could become the stuff of nightmares in a heartbeat.

Alex was blissfully unaware of his tension, though, and kept up a steady stream of comments as they walked toward the bank of elevators. "It's this one," she said and used her key card to activate it.

While they waited, he took another quick look around and noted that no one had paid the slightest attention to them. Good. Seemed that her identity was still a secret. Somehow that made him feel a bit better about his own failure to recognize her.

But in his own defense, you didn't normally see a princess in blue jeans taking a cab to Disneyland.

She was staying in the penthouse suite, of course, and he was glad to see that there was a special elevator for that floor that required a key card. At least she had semiprotection. Not from the hotel staff of course, and he knew how easily bribed a staff member could be. For the right price, some people would sell off their souls.

When the elevator opened, they stepped into a marble-floored entryway with a locked door opposite them. He waited for her to open the door then before she could say anything, he stepped inside, to assure himself that all was as it should be. His practiced gaze swept over the interior of the plushly decorated suite. Midnight-blue couches and chairs made up conversation areas. An unlit fireplace took up most of one wall and the sliding glass doors along a wall of windows afforded an amazing view of the ocean. Starlight filled the dark sky and the moon shone down on the water with a sparkling silver light.

He stalked across the suite to the bedroom, gave it and the master bath a quick, thorough look then moved back into the living room. He checked the balcony then swept his gaze around the room. No sign of anything and just the stillness in the room told him that there hadn't been any intruders.

"What're you doing?" she asked, tossing the key card onto the nearest table.

"Just making sure you're okay." He brushed it off as if it were nothing more than any other guy would have done. But she was no dummy and her blue eyes narrowed slightly in suspicion.

Her nose was sunburned, her hair was a wild tangle and she looked, he thought, absolutely edible. His body stirred in reaction and he told himself to get a grip. There wouldn't be any more kisses. No more fantasies. Not now that he knew who she was.

Alex was strictly off-limits. Oh, he wanted her. Bad. But damned if he was going to start an international incident or something. He'd met her father. He knew the king was not the kind of man to take it lightly if some commoner was sniffing around the royal princess. And Garrett didn't need the extra hassle anyway. Yeah, she was gorgeous. And hot. And funny and smart. But that crown of hers was just getting in the way. And beside all that was the fact that she was here. Alone. Unprotected. Garrett was hardwired to think more of her safety than of his own wants. And mixing the two never worked well.

"Well, I appreciate it," she said softly, "but I'm really

fine. The hotel is a good one and they have excellent security."

Uh-huh. He wasn't so sure of that, but he'd be doing some checking into the situation, that was for damn sure. True, it was a five-star hotel and that usually meant guests were safe. But as he had found out the hard way, mistakes happened.

"Thank you again."

Alex walked toward him and everything in him wanted to reach out, grab her and pull her in close. He could still taste her, damn it, and he knew he wouldn't be forgetting anytime soon just how good she felt, pressed up against him. His body was hard and aching like a bad tooth, which didn't do much for his attitude.

"I had a wonderful day." Her smile widened and she threw her arms out. "Actually, it was perfect. Just as I'd always imagined my first day at Disneyland would be."

That statement caught him off guard and he laughed. "You imagined a five-year-old talking your ears off?"

"I imagined a day spent with friends and finding someone who—" She broke off there, letting the rest of what she might have said die unuttered.

Just as well, Garrett told himself. He might be a professional security expert, but he was also a guy. And knowing that she felt the same pulse of desire he did was almost more than he could take.

Hell, if he didn't get out of there soon, he might forget all about his principles and better judgment.

"Guess I'd better go," he said, stepping past her for the open doorway while he could still manage it.

"Oh. Are you sure?" She waved one hand at the wet bar across the room. "Maybe one drink first? Or I could call room service…"

She wasn't making this easy, he told himself. Need

grabbed him at the base of the throat and squeezed. It would be so easy to stay here. To kiss her again and take his time about it. To feel her body respond to his and to forget all about who she was. Who he was. And why this was a really bad idea.

"I don't think so," he said, "but thanks. Another time."

"Of course." Disappointment clouded her features briefly. And after a day of watching her smile and enjoy herself, damned if he could stand her feeling badly.

"How about breakfast?" He heard himself say it and couldn't call the words back.

That smile of hers appeared again and his heart thudded painfully in his chest. Garrett King, master of bad mistakes.

"I'd like that."

"I'll see you then," he said and stepped out of the penthouse, closing the door quietly behind him.

In the elevator, he stood perfectly still and let the annoying Muzak fill his mind and, temporarily at least, drive out his churning thoughts. But it couldn't last. He had to think about this. Figure out how to handle this situation.

Yes, he wanted Alex.

But his own code of behavior demanded that he protect—not bed—the princess.

He watched the numbers over the elevator doors flash and as they hit the first floor and those doors sighed open, he told himself that maybe he could do both.

The question was, should he?

Three

"Did you and Mickey have a good time?"

"Funny." Garrett dropped into his favorite, bloodred leather chair and propped his feet up on the matching hassock. Clutching his cell phone in one hand and a cold bottle of beer in the other, he listened to his twin's laughter.

"Sorry, man," Griff finally said, "but made me laugh all day thinking about you hauling your ass around the happiest place on Earth. All day. Still can't believe you let Jackson con you into going."

"Wasn't Jackson," Garrett told him. "It was Casey."

"Ah. Well then, that's different." Griffin sighed. "What is it about women? How do they get us to do things we would never ordinarily do?"

"Beats the hell outta me," Garrett said. In his mind, he was seeing Alex again as he said goodbye. Her eyes shining, her delectable mouth curved…

"So was it hideous?"

"What?"

"I swear, when I went to Knott's Berry Farm with them last summer, Mia about wore me into the ground. That kid is like the Tiny Terminator."

"Good description," Garrett agreed with a laugh. "And she was pumped today. Only time she sat down was when we were on a ride."

Sympathy in his tone, Griffin said, "Man, that sounds miserable."

"Would have been."

"Yeah…?"

Garrett took a breath, considered what he was about to do, then went with his gut. He was willing to keep Alex's secret, for the time being anyway, but not from Griffin. Not only were they twins, but they were partners in the security firm they had built together.

"So, talk. Explain what saved you from misery."

"Right to the point, as always," Garrett murmured. His gaze swept the room. His condo wasn't big, but it suited him. He'd tried living in hotels for a while like his cousin Rafe had done for years until meeting his wife, Katie. But hotels got damned impersonal and on the rare occasions when Garrett *wasn't* traveling all over the damn globe, he had wanted a place that was *his*. Something familiar to come home to.

He wasn't around enough to justify a house, and he didn't like the idea of leaving it empty for weeks at a stretch, either. But this condo had been just right. A home that he could walk away from knowing the home owner's association was looking after the property.

It was decorated for comfort, and the minute he walked in, he always felt whatever problems he was thinking about slide away. Maybe it was the view of the ocean.

Maybe it was the knowledge that this was his space, one that no one could take from him. Either way, over the past couple of years, it really had become *home*.

The study where he sat now was a man's room, from the dark paneling to the leather furniture to the stone hearth on the far wall. There were miles of bookshelves stuffed with novels, the classics and several gifts presented to him by grateful clients.

And beyond the glass doors, there was a small balcony where he could stand and watch the water. Just like the view from Alex's hotel room. Amazing how quickly his mind could turn and focus back on her.

"Hello? Garrett? You still there?"

"Yes, I'm here."

"Then talk. No more stalling. What's going on?"

"I met a woman today."

"Well, shout hallelujah and alert the media!" Griffin hooted a laugh that had Garrett wrenching the phone away from his ear. "'Bout time you got lucky. I've been telling you for months you needed to loosen up some. What's she like?"

"Believe me when I say she defies description."

"Right. You met a goddess at Disneyland."

"Not exactly."

"What's that mean?"

"She's a princess."

"Oh, no," Griffin groaned dramatically. "You didn't hook up with some snotty society type, did you? Because that's just wrong."

Frowning, Garrett said, "No, she's a *princess*."

"Now I'm confused. Are we talking a real princess? Crown? Throne?"

"Yep."

"What the—"

"Remember that job we did for the King of Cadria a few years ago?"

Silence, while his brother thought about it, then, "Yeah. I remember. They were doing some big show of the crown jewels and we set up the security for the event. Good job."

"Yeah. Remember the daughter?"

"Hah. Of course I remember her. Never met her face-to-face, but I saw her around the palace from a distance once or twice. Man she was—" Another long pause. "Are you kidding me?"

Garrett had gotten a few of those long-distance glances, too. He remembered not paying much attention to her, either. When he was on a job, his concentration was laser-like. Nothing but security concerns had registered for him and once that had been accomplished, he and his brother had left Cadria.

Since the small island nation was just off the coast of England, he and Griffin had flown to Ireland to visit their cousin Jefferson and his family. And never once had Garrett given the crown princess another thought.

Until today.

"Nope. Not kidding. Princess Alexis was at Disneyland today."

"I didn't see anything about it on the news."

"You won't, either." Garrett took a swig of his beer and hoped the icy brew would cool him off. His body was still thrumming, his groin hot and hard, and he had a feeling it was only going to get worse for him, the longer he spent in her company. "She's hiding out or some damn thing. Told us her name was Alex, that's all."

"What about her security?"

"Doesn't have any that I could see."

Griffin inhaled sharply. "That's not good, bro."

"No kidding?" Garrett shook his head as Griffin's concern flashed his own worries into higher gear. Alex was all alone in a hotel room and *Garrett* was the only one who knew where she was. He couldn't imagine her family allowing her to be unprotected, so that told him she had slipped away from her guards. Which left her vulnerable. Hell, anything could happen to her.

"What're you gonna do about it?"

He checked the time on the grandfather clock on the far wall. "I'm going to wait another hour or so, then I'm calling her father."

Griffin laughed. "Yeah, cuz it's that easy to just pick up a phone and call the palace. Hello, King? This is King."

Garrett rolled his eyes at his brother's lame joke. They'd heard plenty just like that one while they were doing the job for Alex's father. Kings working for kings and all that.

"Why am I talking to you again?"

"Because I'm your twin. The one that got all the brains."

"Must explain why I got all the looks," Garrett muttered with a smile.

"In your dreams."

It was an old game. Since they were identical, neither of them had anything to lose by the insults. Griffin was the one person in his life Garrett could always count on. There were four other King brothers in their branch of the family, and they were all close. But being twins had set Garrett and Griffin apart from the rest of their brothers. Growing up, they'd been a team, standing against their older brothers' teasing. They'd played ball together, learned how to drive together and dated cheerleaders together. They were still looking out for each other.

To Kings, nothing was more important than family. Family came first. Always.

Griffin finally stopped laughing and asked, "Seriously, what are you going to do?"

"Just what I said. I'm going to call her father. He gave us a private number, remember?"

"Oh, right."

Nodding, Garrett said, "First, I want to find out if the king knows where she is."

"You think she ran away?"

"I think she's going to a lot of trouble to avoid having people recognize her, so yeah." He remembered the blue jeans, the simple white shirt, the platform heels and her wild tangle of hair. Nope. Not how anyone would expect a princess to look. "Wouldn't be surprised to find out no one but us knows where she is. Anyway, I'll let the king know she's okay and find out how he wants me to handle this."

"And how do *you* want to handle it?" Griffin asked.

Garrett didn't say a word, which pretty much answered Griffin's question more eloquently than words could have. What could he possibly have said anyway? That he didn't want to handle the situation—he wanted to handle *Alex?* Yeah, that'd be good.

"She must be something else."

"Y'know? She really is," he said tightly. "And she's going to stay safe."

Memories flew around him like a cloud of mosquitoes. Nagging. Irritating. He couldn't stop them. Never had been able to make them fade. And that was as it should be, he told himself. He'd made a mistake and someone had died. He should never be allowed to forget.

"Garrett," Griffin said quietly, "you've got to let the past go."

He winced and took another drink of his beer. As twins, they had always been finely attuned to each other. Not exactly reading each other's minds or anything—thank God for small favors. But there was usually an undercurrent that each of them could pick up on. Clearly, Griffin's twin radar was on alert.

"Who's talking about the past?" Bristling, Garrett pushed haunting memories aside and told himself that Alex's situation had nothing to do with what had happened so long ago. And he would do whatever he could to see that it stayed that way.

"Fine. Be stubborn. Keep torturing yourself for something that you did. Not. Do."

"I'm done talking about it," Garrett told his brother.

"Whatever. Always were a hard head."

"Hello, pot? This is kettle. You're black."

"Hey," Griffin complained, "I'm the funny one, remember?"

"What was I thinking?" Garrett smiled to himself and sipped at his beer.

"Look, just keep me posted on this. Let me know what her father has to say and if you need backup, *call*."

"I will," he promised, even though he knew he wouldn't be calling. He didn't want backup with Alex. He wanted to watch over her himself. He trusted his brother with his life. But he would trust *no one* with Alex's. The only way to make sure she stayed safe was to take care of her himself.

Alex couldn't sleep.

Every time she closed her eyes, her mind dredged up images snatched from her memories of the day. Mostly, of course, images of Garrett—laughing, teasing his nieces, carrying a sleeping baby...and images of him as he leaned in to kiss her.

Oh, that kiss had been...well, way too short, but aside

from that, wonderful. She could still hear the water sloshing against the boat, the singing from the pirates and feel the hot wind buffeting their faces. Still feel his mouth moving over hers.

It had been, she told herself with a small smile, *magic*.

She picked up her hot tea off the room service cart and stepped onto the balcony of her suite. A summer wind welcomed her with the cool kiss of the sea. She stared up at the night sky then shifted her gaze to the ocean where the moon's light danced across the surface of the water, leaving a silvery trail, as if marking a path to be followed. In the middle of the night, everything was quiet, as if the whole world was dreaming.

And if she could sleep, Alex knew her dreams would be filled with Garrett.

She took a sip of the tea and sighed in satisfaction.

Alexis knew she should feel guilty for having left Cadria the way she had, but she just couldn't manage it. Maybe it was because of the years she had spent doing all the "right" things. She had been a dutiful daughter, a helpful sister, a perfect princess. She was always in the right place at the right time saying the right things.

She loved her father, but the man was practically medieval. If it weren't for her mother's restraining influence, King Gregory of Cadria would probably have had his only daughter fitted for a chastity belt and tucked away in a tower. Until he picked out the right husband for her, of course.

Alex had had to fight for every scrap of independence she had found over the past few years. She hadn't wanted to be seen only at state occasions. Or to christen a new ship or open a new park. She wanted more. She wanted her life to mean something.

And if that meant a twenty-eight-year-old woman had to run away from home—then so be it.

She only hoped her father would eventually forgive her. Maybe he would understand one day just how important her independence was to her.

Nothing had ever been *hers*. The palace deemed what she should do and when she should do it.

Even her work with single mothers in need, in the capital city of Cadria, had been co-opted by the palace press. They made her out to be a saint. To be the gently bred woman reaching out to the less fortunate. Which just infuriated her and embarrassed the women she was trying to help.

Her entire life had been built around a sense of duty and privilege, and it was choking her.

Shaking her head, she tried to push that thought aside because she knew very well how pitiful that sounded. Poor little rich girl, such a trying life. But being a princess was every bit as suffocating as she had tried to tell little Mia earlier.

Mia.

Alexis smiled to herself in spite of her rushing thoughts. That little girl and her family had given Alex one of the best days of her life. Back at the palace, she had felt as though her life was slipping away from her, disappearing into the day-to-day repetitiveness of the familiar. The safe.

There were no surprises in her world. No days of pure enjoyment. No rush of attraction or sizzle of sexual heat. Though she had longed for all of those for most of her life.

She had grown up on tales of magic. Romance. Her mom had always insisted that there was something special about Disneyland. That the joy that infused the place somehow made it more enchanted than anywhere else.

Alex's mother had been nineteen and working in one

of the gift shops on Main Street when she met the future King of Cadria. Of course, Mom hadn't known then that the handsome young man flirting with her was a prince. She had simply fallen for his kind eyes and quiet smile. He kept his title a secret until Alex's mother was in love—and that, Alexis had always believed, was the secret. Find a man who didn't know who she was. Someone who would want her for herself, not for who her father was.

Today, she thought, she might have found him. And in the same spot where her own mother had found the magic that changed her life.

"I can't feel guilty because it was worth it," she murmured a moment later, not caring that she was talking to herself. One of the downsides of being by yourself was that you had no one to talk things over with. But the upside was, if she talked to herself instead, there was no one to notice or care.

Her mind drifted back to thoughts of her family and she winced a little as she realized that they were probably worried about her. No doubt her father was half crazed, her mother was working to calm him down and her older brothers were torn between exasperation and pride at what she'd managed to do.

She would call them in a day or two and let them know she was safe. But until then, she was simply going to *be*. For the first time in her life, she was just like any other woman. There was no one to dress her, advise her, hand her the day's agenda. Her time was her own and she had no one to answer to.

Freedom was a heady sensation.

Still, she couldn't believe she had actually gotten away with it. Ditching her personal guards—who she really hoped didn't get into too much trouble with her father— disguising herself, buying an airplane ticket and slipping out of Cadria unnoticed. Her father was no doubt furious, but truth to tell, all of this was really his fault. If he hadn't started making noises about Alex "settling down," finding an "appropriate" husband and taking up her royal duties, then maybe she wouldn't have run.

Not that her father was an ogre, she assured herself. He was really a nice man, but, in spite of the fact that he had married an American woman who had a mind of her own and a spine of steel, he couldn't see that his daughter needed to find her own way.

Which meant that today, she was going to make the most of what she might have found with Garrett—she frowned. God, she didn't even know his last name.

She laughed and shook her head. Names didn't matter. All that mattered was that the stories her mother had told her were true.

"Mom, you were *right*," she said, cradling her cup between her palms, allowing the heat to seep into her. "Disneyland is a special place filled with magic. And I think I found some for myself."

He had already been cleared for the penthouse elevator, so when Garrett arrived early in the morning, he went right up. The hum of the machinery was a white noise that almost drowned out the quiet strains of the Muzak pumping down on him from overhead speakers.

His eyes felt gritty from lack of sleep, but his body was wired. He was alert. Tense. And, he silently admitted, eager to see Alex again.

Stupid, he knew, but there it was. He had no business allowing desire to blind him. She was a princess, for God's sake and he was now, officially, her bodyguard.

Garrett caught his own reflection in the mirrored wall opposite him and scowled. He should have seen it coming, what had happened when he finally got through to the King of Cadria. The fact that he had been surprised only underlined exactly how off course his brain was.

In the seconds it took for the elevator to make its climb, he relived that conversation.

"She's in California?"

The king's thundering shout probably could have been heard even without the telephone.

Well, Garrett told himself, that answered his first question. He had been right. The king had had no idea where Alex was.

"Is she safe?"

"Yes," Garrett said quickly as his measure of the king went up a notch or two. Sure he was pissed, but he was also more concerned about his daughter's safety than anything else. "She's safe, but she's on her own. I'm not comfortable with that."

"Nor am I, Mr. King."

"Garrett, please."

"Garrett, then." He muttered to someone in the room with him, "Yes, yes, I will ask, give me a moment, Teresa," he paused, then said, "Pardon me. My wife is very concerned for Alexis, as are we all."

"I understand." In fact Garrett was willing to bet that "very concerned" was a major understatement.

"So, Garrett. My wife wished to know how you found Alexis."

"Interestingly enough, I was with my family at Disneyland," he said, still amused by it all. Imagine stumbling across a runaway princess in the heart of an amusement park. "We met outside one of the rides."

No point telling the king that Garrett had come to Alex's rescue, not knowing who she was. No point in mention-

ing the kiss he had stolen in the darkness of a pirate ride, either.

"I knew it!" The king shouted then spoke to his wife in the room with him. "Teresa, this is your fault, filling our daughter's head with romantic nonsense until she—"

Listening in on a royal argument just underscored what Garrett had learned long ago. People were people. Didn't matter if they wore a king's crown or a baseball cap. They laughed, they fought, they cried—all of them. And it sounded to Garrett that the King of Cadria, like any other man, didn't have a clue how to deal with women.

The king's voice broke off and a moment later a soft, feminine voice spoke up. The queen, Garrett guessed, and smiled as he realized that she clearly didn't let her husband's blustering bother her.

"Hello, Garrett?"

"Yes, ma'am."

"Is Alexis well?"

"Yes, ma'am, as I told your husband, she was fine when I took her back to her hotel last night."

"Oh, that's such good news, thank you. You say you met her at Disneyland?"

"Yes, ma'am."

More to herself than to him, the queen murmured, "She always dreamed of visiting the park. I should have guessed she would go there, but—"

A princess dreaming about Disneyland. Well, other young girls dreamed of being a princess, so he supposed it made sense. Garrett heard the worry in the queen's voice and he wondered if Alex was even the slightest bit concerned about what her family was going through.

"Thank you again for looking out for my daughter," the queen said, "and now, my husband wants to speak to you again."

Garrett smiled to himself imagining the phone shuffle going on in a palace a few thousand miles away. When the king came back on the line, his tone was quieter.

"Yes, my dear, you're right. Of course. Garrett?"

"I'm here, sir."

"I would like to hire you to protect our daughter."

Instantly, Garrett did a quick mental step backward. This wasn't what he'd had in mind. He didn't want to guard her body. He just wanted her. Not the best basis for a protection detail.

"I don't think that's a good idea—"

"We will pay whatever you ask, but frankly my wife feels that Alexis needs this time to herself so I can't very well drag her back home, much as I would prefer it. At the same time, I'm unwilling to risk her safety."

Good point, Garrett couldn't help but admit. Whether she thought so or not, there was potential danger all around Alexis. Which is why he had placed this call in the first place. He thought she should be protected—just not by him. "I agree that the princess needs a bodyguard, but..."

"Excellent." The king interrupted him neatly. "You will keep us informed of what she's doing, where she's going?"

Instantly, Garrett bristled. That wasn't protection; that was being an informant. Not once in all the years he and his twin had run their agency had they resorted to snapping pictures of cheating spouses and damned if he was going to start down that road now.

"I'm not interested in being a spy, your majesty."

A dismissive chuckle sounded. "A spy. This isn't the situation at all. I'm asking that you protect my daughter—for a handsome fee—and along the way that you merely observe and report. What, Teresa?" Garrett heard furious whispers during the long pause and finally the king came back on the line. "Fine, it is spying. Very well. Observe and not report?"

He still didn't like it. Then the king spoke again.

"Garrett, my daughter wants her holiday, but she's managed to lose every guard I've ever assigned her. We would appreciate it very much if you would watch over Alexis."

Which was why he had finally agreed to this.

Garrett came back out of his memories with a thoughtful frown at his image. He had the distinct feeling that this was not going to end well.

But what the hell else was he supposed to do? Tell a man, a king, that he *wouldn't* protect his daughter? And still, he would have refused outright if the king had insisted on the spying.

But damned if he could think of a way to get out of guarding her. The king didn't want Alex's presence announced to the world, for obvious reasons, and since Garrett had already met her, and was a trained security specialist besides, how could he *not* take the assignment?

If he had said no and something happened to Alexis, he'd never be able to live with himself. His frown deepened as he silently admitted that the truth was, he already had one dead girl haunting him—he wouldn't survive another.

Four

At the knock on her door, Alex opened it and smiled up at Garrett.

The slam of what she had felt around him the day before came back harder and faster than ever. He was so tall. Broad shoulders, narrow hips. He wore black jeans, a dark green pullover shirt—open at the collar, with short sleeves that displayed tanned, muscular forearms. His boots were scuffed and well worn, just adding to the whole "danger" mystique. His features were stark, but somehow beautiful. His eyes shone like a summer sky and the mouth she had thought about way too often was quirked in a half smile.

"I'm impressed."

"You are?" she asked. "With what?"

"You're ready to go," he said, sweeping his gaze up and down her before meeting her gaze again. "Not going to have me sit in the living room while you finish your hair or put on makeup or decide what to wear?"

Her eyebrows lifted. He had no way of knowing of course, but she had been raised to be punctual. The King of Cadria never kept people waiting and he expected the same of his family.

"Well," she said, "that was completely sexist. Good morning to you, too."

He grinned, obviously unapologetic. "Wasn't meant to be sexist, merely grateful," he said, stepping past her into the living room of her suite. "I hate waiting around while a woman drags her feet just so she can make an entrance." He gave her a long, slow look, then said, "Although, you would have been worth the wait."

She flushed with pleasure. A simple compliment simply given, and it meant so much more than the flowery stuff she was used to hearing. As for "entrances," she got way too many of those when she was at home. People standing when she entered a room, crowds thronging for a chance at a handshake or a photo. A band striking up when she was escorted into a formal affair.

And none of those experiences gave her the same sort of pleasure she found in seeing Garrett's reaction to her. Alex threw her hair back over her shoulder and tugged at the hem of her short-sleeved, off-the-shoulder, dark red shirt. She had paired the top with white slacks and red, sky-high heels that gave her an extra three inches in height. Yet still she wasn't at eye level with Garrett.

And the gleam in his eyes sent pinpricks of expectation dancing along her skin. Funny, she'd been awake half the night, but Alex had never felt more alert. More...alive. She should have done this years ago, she thought. Striking out on her own. Going incognito, meeting people who had no idea who she was. But then, even as those thoughts raced through her mind, she had to admit, if only to herself, that the real reason she was feeling so wired wasn't her little holiday. It was Garrett.

She'd never known a man like him. Gorgeous, yes. But there was more to him than the kind of face that should be on the pages of a magazine. There was his laughter, his kindness to his little cousins—and the fact that he'd ridden to her rescue.

And the fact that the black jeans he wore looked amazing on him didn't hurt anything, either.

Alex watched him now as he scanned the perimeter of the room as if looking for people hiding behind the couches and chairs. Frowning slightly, she realized that she'd seen a similar concentrated, laserlike focus before. From the palace guards and her own personal protection detail. He had the air of a man on a mission. As if it were his *job* to keep her safe. Doubt wormed its way through her mind.

Was it possible this had all been a setup? Had her father somehow discovered her whereabouts and sent Garrett to watch over her?

Then she silently laughed and shook her head at the thought. Garrett had been at Disneyland with his family. Their meeting was accidental. Serendipity. She was reading too much into this, letting her imagination spiral out of control. Alex was projecting her concerns onto Garrett's presence with absolutely no reason at all to do so. The man was simply looking around the penthouse suite.

She was so used to staying in hotels like this one she tended to forget that not everyone in the world was blasé about a penthouse. Inwardly smiling at the wild turns paranoia could take, she ordered herself to calm down and patiently waited for Garrett's curiosity to be satiated.

Finally, he turned to look at her, his features unreadable. "So. Breakfast?"

"Yes, thanks. I'm starving."

He gave her that grin that seemed designed to melt her knees and leave her sprawling on the rug. Really, the man had a presence that was nearly overpowering.

"Another thing I like about you, Alex. You admit when you're hungry."

She shook off the sexual hunger clawing at her and smiled back at him. "Let me guess, most women you know don't eat?"

He shrugged as if the women in his life meant nothing and she really hoped that was the case.

"Let's just say the ones I've known consider splitting an M&M a hearty dessert."

She laughed at the image. "I know some women like that, too," she said, snatching up her red leather bag off the closest chair. "I've never understood it. Me, I love to eat."

"Good to know," he said, one corner of his mouth lifting.

And there went the swirl of something hot and delicious in the pit of her stomach. How was she supposed to keep a lid on her imagination if every look and smile he gave her set off incendiary devices inside her?

This holiday was becoming more interesting every minute. When he took her hand and drew her from the penthouse, Alex savored the heat of his skin against hers and told herself to stop overthinking everything and just enjoy every moment she was with him.

They had breakfast down the coast in Laguna Beach, at a small café on Pacific Coast Highway. On one side of the patio dining area, the busy street was clogged with cars and the sidewalks bustled with pedestrian traffic. On the other side, the Pacific Ocean stretched out to the horizon. Seagulls wheeled and dipped in the air currents, surfers rode waves in to shore and pleasure boats bobbed lazily on the water. And Alex was only vaguely aware of any of it. How could she be distracted by her surroundings when she could hardly take her eyes off Garrett? His thick, black hair lifted in a capricious breeze and she nearly sighed when he reached up to push his hair off his forehead. The man was completely edible, she thought, and wondered vaguely what he might look like in a suit. Probably just as gorgeous, she decided silently, but she preferred him like this. There were too many suits in her world.

This man was nothing like the other men in her life. Which was only one of the reasons he so intrigued her.

But Garrett seemed…different this morning. Less relaxed, somehow, although that was probably perfectly natural. People were bound to be more casual and laid-back at an amusement park than they were in everyday situations. The interesting part was she liked him even more now.

There was something about his air of casual danger that appealed to her. Not that she was afraid of him in any way, but the sense of tightly reined authority bristling off him said clearly that he was in charge and no one with him had to worry about a thing.

She laughed to herself. Funny, but the very thing she found so intriguing about him was what drove her the craziest about her father.

"Want to share the joke?" he asked, that deep voice of his rumbling along every single one of her nerve endings.

"No," she said abruptly. "Not really."

"Okay, but when a woman is chuckling to herself, a man always assumes she's laughing at *him*."

"Oh, I doubt that." Alex reached for her coffee cup and took a sip. When she set it down again, she added, "I can't imagine too many women laugh at you."

Amusement sparkled in his eyes. "Never more than once."

Now she did laugh and he gave her a reluctant smile.

"Not intimidated by me at all, are you?" he asked.

"Should I be?"

"Most people are."

"I'm not most people."

"Yeah," he said wryly, "I'm getting that." He leaned back in his chair and asked, "So what next, Alex? Anything else on your 'must see' list besides Disneyland?"

She grinned. It was wonderful. Being here. Alone. With him. No palace guards in attendance. No assistants or ministers or parents or brothers hovering nearby. She felt freer than she ever had and she didn't want to waste a moment of it. Already, her excitement had a bittersweet tinge to it because Alex knew this time away from home couldn't last.

All too soon, she would have to go back to Cadria. Duty was far too ingrained in her to allow for a permanent vacation. Another week was probably all she could manage before she would have to return and be Princess Alexis again. At the thought, she almost heard the palace doors close behind her. Almost sensed the weight of her crown pressing against her forehead. *Poor little rich girl,* she thought wryly and briefly remembered Garrett's tiny cousin wistfully dreaming of being a princess.

If only the little girl could realize that what she already had was worth so much more. A ripple of regret washed through Alex as she turned her gaze on the busy street.

She wondered how many of the people laughing, talking, planning a lazy day at the beach were like her—on holiday and already dreading the return to their real world.

"Alex?"

She turned her head to look at him and found his gaze locked on her. "Sorry. Must have been daydreaming."

"Didn't look like much of a daydream. What's got you frowning?"

He was far too perceptive, she thought and warned herself to guard her emotions more closely. "Just thinking that I don't want my holiday to end."

"Everything ends," he said quietly. "The trick is not to worry about the ending so much that you don't enjoy what you've got while you've got it."

Nodding, she said, "You're absolutely right."

"I usually am," he teased. "Ask anybody."

"You're insufferable, aren't you?"

"Among many other things," he told her, and she felt a tug of something inside her when his mouth curved just the slightest bit.

Then he turned his back on the busy street and looked out at the water. She followed his gaze, and nearly sighed at the perfection of the view. Tiny, quick-footed birds dashed in and out of the incoming tide. Lovers walked along the shore and children built castles in the sand.

Castles.

She sighed a little at the reminder of her daydream, of the world waiting for her return.

"So no big plans for today then?" he asked.

"No," she said with a suddenly determined sigh, "just to see as much as I can. To enjoy the day."

"Sounds like a good idea to me. How about we explore the town a little then take a drive along the coast?"

Relief sparkled inside her. She had been sure he'd have to leave. Go to work. Do whatever he normally did when not spending time with a runaway princess. "Really? That sounds wonderful. If you're sure you don't have to be somewhere…"

"I'm all yours," he said, spreading his arms as if offering himself to her.

And ooh, the lovely sizzle that thought caused. "You don't have to be at work?"

"Nope. I'm taking a few days off."

"Well, then, lucky me."

The waitress approached with the check, Garrett pulled a few bills from his wallet and handed them to her.

"Hmm, that reminds me," Alex said when the woman was gone again. "You owe me five dollars."

His eyebrows lifted. "For what?"

She folded her arms on the table. "We had a wager yesterday and you never did guess where I'm from."

He nodded, gaze locked on hers, and warmth dazzled her system. Honestly, if he were to reach out and touch her while staring at her as he was, Alex was sure she'd simply go up in flames.

"So we did," he said and reached into his wallet again.

"You don't have to actually pay me," she said, reaching out to stop him. Her hand touched his and just as she'd suspected, heat surged through her like an out of control wildfire. She pulled her hand back quickly, but still the heat lingered. "I just wanted you to admit you lost. You did buy breakfast after all."

"I always pay my debts," he said and pulled out a five. Before he could hand it over, though, Alex dug into her purse for a pen and gave it to him. "What's this for?"

"Sign it," she said with a shrug and a smile. "That way I'll always remember winning my first wager."

He snorted an unexpected laugh. "That was your first bet?"

No one but her brothers—and they didn't count—ever made bets with a princess. It would be considered tacky. A tiny sigh escaped her before she could stop it. How much she had missed just because of how things might "look."

"You're my first—outside my family of course. And I did pretty well, I think, don't you? I did earn five dollars."

"So you did," he said, clearly amused. "Okay then..." He took her pen, scrawled a message, signed it and handed both the pen and the money to her.

Alex looked down and read, "Payment in full to Alex from Garrett." She lifted her gaze, cocked her head and said, "I still don't know your last name."

He nodded. "Don't know yours, either."

"Seems odd, don't you think?" Her gaze dropped to his signature. It was bold, strong and she had no doubt that a handwriting analyst would say that Garrett was confident, powerful and even a little arrogant.

"I'll tell you my name if you tell me yours," he taunted.

Her gaze snapped to his. Tell him her last name? She considered it for a second or two. Wells was common enough; maybe he wouldn't think anything of it. But then again, if he put her first name with her last, it might ring a familiar bell that she'd rather remain silent.

She was having too much fun as "just Alex" to want to give it up this early in her holiday. So why risk it? Why insist on last names when it didn't really matter anyway? After all, when her holiday was over, they'd never see each other again. Wasn't it better for both of them to keep things light? Superficial?

He was still watching her. Waiting. She couldn't read his expression and she really wished she could. Alex would have loved to know what he was thinking about this...whatever it was between them. If he was as intrigued, as filled with a heightened sense of anticipation as she was.

"So?" he asked, a half smile curving his mouth as he waited for her decision.

"First names only," she said with an emphatic nod. "It's more fun that way, don't you agree?"

"I think," Garrett said as he stood up and held one hand out to her, "the fun hasn't even started yet."

"Is that a promise?" she asked, slipping her hand into his and relishing the rush of heat and lust that immediately swamped her.

"It is," he said, "and I always keep my promises."

Garrett looked down at their joined hands then lifted his gaze to hers as the buzz between them sizzled and snapped like sparks lifting off a bonfire. "Fun. Coming right up."

They spent a couple of hours in Laguna, wandering down the sidewalks, drifting in and out of the eclectic mix of shops lining Pacific Coast Highway. There were art galleries, handmade ice cream parlors, jewelry stores and psychics. There were street performers, entertaining for the change dropped into open guitar cases and there were tree-shaded benches where elderly couples sat and watched the summer world roll by.

Alex was amazing. She never got tired, never got bored and absolutely everything caught her attention. She talked to everyone, too. It was as if she was trying to suck up as much life as possible. And he knew why. Soon she'd be going back behind palace walls and the freedom she was feeling at the moment would disappear.

Hard to blame her for wanting to escape. Who the hell didn't occasionally think about simply dropping off the radar and getting lost for a while? He'd done it himself after—Garrett shut that thought down fast. He didn't want to relive the past. Had no interest in wallowing in the pain and guilt that had ridden him so hard for so long. There was nothing to be gained by remembering. He'd learned his lesson, he assured himself, and that was why he was sticking to Alex like glue.

It had nothing to do with how she looked in those mile-high heels. Or the brilliance of her smile or the damn sparkle in her eyes.

He could tell himself whatever he wanted to, he thought, but even *he* didn't believe the lies.

"You're frowning," she said, snapping him out of his thoughts. He was pitifully grateful for the distraction.

"What?"

"Frowning," she repeated. "You. Do I look that hideous?"

He shook his head at the ridiculousness of the question, but dutifully looked at the drawing the caricature artist was doing of Alex. The guy had an easel set up under one of the trees along the highway and boxes of colored pastels sat at his elbow. Garrett watched him drawing and approved of the quick, sure strokes he made.

Alex was coming alive on the page, her smile wider, her eyes bigger and brighter and her long blond hair swirling in an unseen wind.

"So?" she asked.

"It looks great," he muttered, not really caring for how the artist had defined Alex's breasts and provided ample cleavage in the drawing.

"Thanks, man," the guy said, layering in a deeper blue to Alex's eyes. "I love faces. They fascinate me. Like you," he said to Alex, "your face is familiar, somehow. Like I've seen you before. But with that accent no way you're from around here."

Garrett's gaze snapped to her in time to see her face pale a bit and her eyes take on a wary sheen.

"I'm sure I've just got one of 'those' faces," she said, trying to make light of the guy's statement. "You know they say we all have a double out there, wandering the world."

"Yeah," the artist murmured, not really listening. "But you're different. You're…"

"You done?" Garrett asked abruptly.

"Huh?" The guy glanced up at him and whatever he saw in Garrett's eyes convinced him that he was indeed finished. "Sure. Let me just sign it."

A fast scrawl with a black chalk and he was tearing the page off the easel and handing it to Alex. She looked at it and grinned, obviously pleased with the results. In fact, she was so entranced by the drawing, she didn't notice the artist's eyes suddenly widen and his mouth drop open in shock.

Apparently, Garrett thought grimly, he'd finally remembered where he had seen Alex before. Moving fast, Garrett caught the other man's eye and gave him a warning glare that carried threats of retribution if he so much as said a single word.

His meaning got across with no problem. The tall, thin man with the straggly beard closed his mouth, wiped one hand across the back of his neck and nodded in silent agreement.

Garrett pulled out his wallet and handed over a wad of cash. Way more than the price of the drawing, this was also shut-the-hell-up-and-forget-you-ever-saw-her money. When the guy whistled low and long, Garrett knew the bribe was successful.

"Thank you!" Alex said and finally looked at the artist. "It's wonderful. I know just where I'll hang it when I get home."

"Yeah?" The artist grinned, obviously loving the idea that one of his drawings would soon be hanging in a castle.

"Well, cool. Glad you like it, Pr—" He stopped, shot a look at Garrett and finished up lamely, *"Miss."*

Alex missed the man's slipup. She reached into her purse. "How much do I owe you?"

"It's taken care of," Garrett said, stepping up beside her and dropping one arm around her shoulders. He shot another warning look at the artist. "Isn't it?"

"You bet," the guy said, nodding so hard Garrett half expected the man's head to fly off his neck. "All square. We're good. Thanks again."

Garrett steered her away from the artist, and got her walking toward where he'd parked his car. Best to get out of here before the guy forgot just how threatening Garrett could be and started bragging about how he had drawn the portrait of a princess.

"You didn't have to buy this for me, Garrett," she said, with a quick glance up at him. "I appreciate it, but it wasn't necessary."

"I know that. I wanted to."

"Well, I love it." She turned her head to study the portrait. "Whenever I look at it, I'll think of today and what a lovely time I had. I'll remember the ocean, the ice cream, the tide pools, the shops…"

She came to a stop and the people on the sidewalk moved past them like water rushing around a rock in a fast moving stream. She looked at him, reached up and cupped his cheek in her palm. He felt her touch all the way to his bones.

Her blue eyes shone with the glitter of promises when she said, "And I'll remember *you* most of all."

He knew with a soul-deep certainty that he'd never forget her, either.

Five

Decker King looked more like a beach bum than a successful businessman. And that was just how he liked it.

Garrett only shook his head while Decker flirted like crazy with Alex. Decker wore board shorts, flip flops and a T-shirt that read, Do it With a King.

And in smaller letters, King's Kustom Krafts.

The man might be annoying, but his company built the best luxury pleasure crafts in the world. His specialty was the classic, 1940s style wooden powerboats. Decker had customers all over the world sitting on waiting lists for one of his launches.

"You sure you want Garrett to take you out?" Decker was saying, giving Alex a smile meant to seduce.

"Yeah," Garrett interrupted. "She's sure."

Decker glanced at him and smirked. "Okay, then. My personal boat is moored at the dock out back." He tossed the keys to Garrett. "Don't scratch it."

"Thank you, Decker," Alex said with a smile as Garrett grabbed her hand and headed for the dock.

"My pleasure, Alex," he called back as she was hustled away. "Anytime you get tired of my dull cousin, just call me!"

"I don't think you're dull," Alex said on a laugh, her hand tightening around his.

"Decker thinks anyone with a regular job is dull. He's talented but he's also a flake."

"But he runs this business…"

"Yeah, like I said, talented. He's like a savant."

Alex laughed again as they stepped out into the sunlight, leaving the airy boat-building warehouse behind. "Oh, come on. He's very sweet."

"All women like Decker." Garrett looked down at her and smiled. "None of the cousins have figured out why, yet."

"None of you? How many cousins do you have?"

"I can't count that high," he said with a half laugh. "We're all over California. Like a biblical plague."

She laughed and Garrett let the sound ripple over him like sunlight on the water.

"Must be nice, having that much family."

"It can be," he admitted. "It can also be a pain in the ass from time to time."

They stopped at the end of the dock, and Garrett helped her into the sleek boat waiting for them. He untied the rope, tossed it aside then jumped in beside her. The wood planks of the hull gleamed a dark red-brown from layers of varnish and careful polishing. The red leather bench seats were soft and the engine, when Garrett fired it up, sounded like the purr of a mighty beast.

Alex laughed in delight and Garrett couldn't help grinning in response. In a few minutes, he was out of the harbor and headed for open water.

"I love this boat," she shouted over the engine noise. "It's like the ones in that Indiana Jones movie!"

"I love that you know that!" He grinned and gunned the engine harder, bringing the bow up to slap at the water as they careened across the surface.

When they were far enough out that Garrett was convinced that Alex was perfectly safe, he eased back on the throttle. The roar of the engine became a vibrating purr as the sleek powerboat shifted from a wild run into a lazy prowl.

Garrett slanted a look at her. "So, action movie fan are you?"

"Oh, yes." She turned her face up to the sun, closed her eyes and smiled. "It's having three brothers, I think. They had no time for comedies or romance, so movie night at our house meant explosions and gunfire."

"Sounds like my house," he said, remembering the many nights he and his brothers had spent reveling in movie violence. Garrett and Griffin especially had enjoyed the cops and robbers movies. The good guys tracking down the bad guys and saving the day in the end. Maybe that was why he and his twin had both ended up in the security business.

"You have brothers?"

"Four—one of them is my twin."

"A twin! I always thought it would be wonderful to be a twin. Was it?"

"Wonderful?" He shook his head. "Never really thought about it, I guess. But yeah, I suppose so. Especially when we were kids. There was always someone there to listen. To play with and, later, to raise hell with."

Being a twin was such a part of who and what he was

that he'd never really considered what it must look like from the outside. Griffin and he had done so much together, always right there, covering each other's backs that Garrett couldn't imagine *not* being a twin.

"Did you? Raise a lot of hell?"

"Our share," he mused, lost briefly in memories of parties, football games and women. "When we were kids, being identical was just fun. Swapping classes, tricking teachers. As we got older, the fun got a little more…creative."

"Identical?" She took a long look at him. "You're exactly alike?"

He shook his head and gave her a half smile. "Nah. I'm the good-looking one."

She laughed as he'd hoped she would.

"Must have been nice," she said, "raising a little hell once in a while. Having someone to have fun with."

"No hell-raising in your house?" he asked, though he couldn't imagine her and her brothers throwing any wild parties when the king and queen were out of town.

"Not that you'd notice," she said simply, then changed the subject. "Decker seemed very nice." She ran her fingertips across the small brass plaque on the gleaming teak dashboard. *King's Kustom Krafts*.

"Decker King is his name?"

"Yeah." He hadn't even considered that she would learn Decker's last name. And what kind of thing was that for a man like him to admit? Hell, he made his living by always thinking three steps ahead. By knowing what he was going to do long before he actually did it. By being able to guess at what might happen so that his clients were always safe. But around Alex, his brain wasn't really functioning. Nope, it was a completely different part of his body that was in charge now.

And it was damned humbling to admit he couldn't seem to get his blood flowing in the direction of his mind.

"Yeah. Decker's okay."

"He builds lovely boats."

"He really does," Garrett said, relaxing again when she didn't comment on Decker's last name. "So, you've heard about my family, tell me about these brothers of yours."

She looked at him and he read the wary suspicion in her eyes. "Why?"

"Curiosity." He shrugged and shifted his gaze to the sea. No other boats around. But for the surfers closer to shore, they were completely alone. Just the way he preferred it. Giving her a quick glance he saw her gaze was still fixed on him as if she were trying to make up her mind how much to say.

Finally, though, she sighed and nodded. "I've already told you I've got three brothers. They're all older than me. And very bossy." She turned her face into the wind and her long blond hair streamed out behind her. "In fact, they're much like my father in that regard. Always trying to order me about."

"Maybe they're just looking out for you," he said, mentally pitying the brothers Alex no doubt drove nuts. After all, the king himself had told Garrett that Alex managed to lose whatever bodyguards were assigned to her. He could only imagine that she made the lives of her brothers even crazier.

"Maybe they should realize I can look after myself." She shook her head and folded her arms over her chest in such a classic posture of self-protection that Garrett almost smiled.

But damned if he didn't feel bad for her in a way, too. He hated the idea of someone else running his life. Why should she be any different? Still, every instinct he possessed had him siding with her brothers and her father. Wasn't he here, protecting her, because he hadn't been able to stand the idea of her being on her own and vulnerable?

"Guys don't think like that," he told her. "It's got nothing to do with how capable they think you are. Men look out for our families. At least the decent guys do."

"And making us crazy while you do it?"

"Bonus," he said, grinning.

Her tense posture eased as she gave him a reluctant smile. "You're impossible."

"Among many other things," he agreed. Then, since he had her talking, he asked more questions. Maybe he could get her to admit who she was. Bring the truth out herself. *And then what?* Was he going to confess that he already knew? That her father was now *paying* him to spend time with her? Yeah, that'd go over well. How the hell had he gotten himself into this hole anyway?

Disgusted, he blew out a breath and asked, "So, you've got bossy brothers. What about your parents? What're they like?"

She frowned briefly and shifted her gaze back to the choppy sea, focusing on the foam of the whitecaps as if searching for the words she needed. Finally, on a sigh, she said, "They're lovely people, really. And I love them terribly. But they're too entrenched in the past to see that their way isn't the only way."

"Sound like normal parents to me," he mused. "At least, sounds like my dad. He was always telling us how things had been in his day, giving us advice on what we should do, who we should be."

She tucked her hair behind her ears and, instantly, it blew free again. Garrett was glad. He was getting very fond of that wild, tangled mane of curls.

"My parents don't understand that I want to do something different than what they've planned for me."

He imagined exactly what the royal couple had in mind for their only daughter and he couldn't picture it having anything to do with boat trips, ice cream and Disneyland. He knew enough about the life Alex lived to know that she would be in a constant bubble of scrutiny. How she dressed, what she said and who she said it to would be put under a microscope. Reporters would follow her everywhere and her slightest slip would be front page news. Her parents no doubt wanted her safely tucked behind palace walls. And damned if he could blame them for it.

"Give me an example," he said, steering the boat along the coastline. More surfers were gathered at the breakers and, on shore, towels were scattered across the sand like brightly colored jewels dropped by a careless hand.

"All right," she said and straightened her shoulders as if preparing to defend her position. Her voice was stronger, colored with the determination she felt to run her own life. "At home, I volunteer with a program for single mothers."

Her expression shifted, brightening, a smile curving her mouth. Enthusiasm lit up her eyes until they shone like a sunlit lake. When she started talking, he could hear pride in her voice along with a passion that stirred something inside him.

"Many of the women in the program simply need a little help in finding work or day care for their children," she said. "There are widows or divorcées who are trying to get on their feet again." Her eyes softened as she added, "But there are others. Girls who left school to have their babies and now don't have the tools they'll need to support themselves. Young women who've been abused or abandoned and have nowhere to turn.

"At the center, we offer parenting classes, continuing

education courses and a safe day care for the kids. These young women arrive, worried about the future and when they leave, they're ready to take on the world. It's amazing, really."

She turned on the bench seat, tucked one leg beneath her and rested one arm along the back of the seat. Facing him, she looked him in the eye and said, "The program has grown so much in the past couple of years. We've accomplished so many things and dozens of women are now able to care for their children and themselves. A few of our graduates have even taken jobs in the program to give back what they've received."

"It sounds great."

She smiled to herself and he saw the well-earned pride she felt. "It is, and it feels *good* to do something to actually help, you know? To step outside myself and really make a difference."

"Sounds like you're doing a good thing," Garrett said quietly.

"Thank you." She shrugged, but her smile only brightened. "I really feel as though I'm doing something important. These women have taught me so much, Garrett. They're scared and alone. But so brave, too. And being involved with the program is something I've come to love. On my own."

She sighed then and beneath the pride in her voice was a wistfulness that tore at him. "But my parents, sadly, don't see it that way. They're happy for me to volunteer—organizing fundraisers and writing checks. But they don't approve of me donating my time. They want me in the family business and don't want me, as they call it, 'splitting my focus.'"

"They're wrong," he said and cut back enough on the throttle so that they were more drifting now than actually motoring across the water. "You are making a difference. My mom could have used a program like that."

"Your mother?"

Garrett gave her a small smile. "Oh, my mom was one of the most stubborn people on the face of the planet. When she got pregnant with my brother Nathan, she didn't tell our father."

"Why ever not?"

"Always told us later that she wanted to be sure he loved *her*." He smiled to himself, remembering the woman who had been the heart of their family. "She was alone and pregnant. No job skills. She supported herself working at In and Out Burgers. Then, a week before Nathan was born, my father showed up."

"Was he angry?"

"You could say that." Garrett laughed. "Mom insisted later that when he walked into the burger joint and shouted her name, there was steam coming out of his ears."

Alex laughed at the image.

"Dad demanded that she leave with him and get married. Mom told him to either buy a burger or get out of line and go away."

"What did he do?"

"What any man in my family would do," Garrett mused, thinking about the story he and his brothers had heard countless times growing up. "He demanded to see the owner and when the guy showed up, Dad bought the place."

"He bought the *restaurant?*"

"Yep." Grinning now, Garrett finished by saying, "He wrote the guy a check on the spot and the first thing he did as new owner? He fired my mother. Then he picked her up, carried her, kicking and screaming the whole way, to the closest courthouse and married her."

He was still smiling to himself when Alex sighed, "Your father's quite the romantic."

"More like hardheaded and single-minded," Garrett told her with a rueful shake of his head. "The men in our family know what they want, go after it and don't let anything get in their way. Well, except for my uncle Ben. He didn't marry *any* of the mothers of his kids."

"Any?" she asked. "There were a lot of them?"

"Oh, yeah," Garrett said. "That branch of the family still isn't sure they've met all of the half brothers that might be out there."

"I don't even know what to say to that," she admitted.

"No one does."

"Still, passion is hard to ignore," she told him, then asked, "are your parents still that way together?"

"They were," he said softly. "They did everything together. Even dying. We lost them about five years ago in a car accident. Drunk driver took them out when they were driving through the south of France."

"Garrett, I'm so sorry." She laid one hand on his arm and the touch of her fingers sent heat surging through him as surely as if he'd been struck by lightning.

He covered her hand with his and something…indefinable passed between them. Something that had him backing off, fast. He let her go and eased out from under her touch. "Thanks, but after the shock passed, all of us agreed that it was good that they had died together. Neither of them would have been really happy without the other."

"At least you have some wonderful memories. And your family."

"Yeah, I do. But you're lucky to still have your parents in your life. Even if they do make you nuts."

"I know," she said with a determined nod. "I just wish I could make them understand that—" She broke off and laughed. "Never mind. I'm wasting a lovely day with complaints. So I'm finished now."

Whatever he might have said went unspoken when he heard the approach of another boat. Garrett turned to look and saw a speedboat seemingly headed right for them. As casually as he could manage, he steered their boat in the opposite direction and stepped on the gas, putting some distance between them.

"What's wrong?"

He glowered briefly because he hadn't thought she was paying close attention to what he was doing. "Nothing's wrong. Just keeping my distance from that boat."

She looked over her shoulder at the boat that was fading into the distance. "Why? What're you worried about?"

"Everything," he admitted, swinging the little boat around to head back toward shore.

"Well, don't," she said and reached out to lay one hand on his forearm again. The heat from before had hardly faded when a new blast of blistering warmth shot through him. Instantly, his groin tightened and he was forced to grind his teeth together and clench his hands around the wheel to keep from shutting the damn engine off and grabbing her.

Seriously, he hadn't been this tempted by a woman in years.

Maybe never.

Shaking his head at the thought, he said, "Don't what?"

"Don't *worry,* Garrett." She released him and even with the heat of the sun pouring down on them, his skin felt suddenly cool now at the loss of her touch. "I'm taking a holiday from worry and so should you."

That wasn't going to happen. Garrett made his living worrying about possibilities. About danger around every corner. Possible assassins everywhere. Not an easy thing to turn off, and he wasn't sure he would even if he could.

"And what do you usually worry about?" he asked.

"Everything," she said, throwing his own word back at him. "But as I said, I'm taking a holiday. And so are you."

Then she laughed and tipped her face up to the sky. Closing her eyes, she sighed and said, "This is wonderful. The sea, the sun, this lovely boat and—"

"And—?"

She looked over at him. "You."

He nearly groaned. Her blue eyes were wide, her lush mouth curved and that off-the-shoulder blouse of hers was displaying *way* too much off-the-shoulder for his sanity's sake. Now it had dipped low over her left shoulder, baring enough of her chest that he could only think about getting the damn fabric down another two or three inches.

For God's sake, she was killing him without even trying. Garrett was forced to remind himself that he was on a job here. He was working for her father. It was his job to *guard* her luscious body, not *revel* in it.

Besides, if she knew the truth, knew who he was and that her father was paying him to spend time with her... hell, she'd probably toss his ass off the boat and then drive it over him just for good measure.

Knowing that didn't change a damn thing, though. He still wanted her. Bad.

"Alex..."

"I've been thinking." She slid closer. Their thighs were brushing now and he felt the heat of her through the layers of fabric separating them.

He almost didn't ask, but he had to. "About what?"

"That kiss."

Briefly, he closed his eyes. Throttling back, he cut the engine and the sudden silence was overwhelming. All they heard was the slap of water against the hull, the sigh of the wind across the ocean and the screech of seagulls wheeling in air currents overhead.

That kiss.

Oh, he'd been thinking about it, too. About what he would have done if they'd been alone in the dark and not surrounded by laughing kids and harassed parents. In fact, he'd already invested far too much time indulging his fantasies concerning Alex. So much so that if she moved another inch closer…pressed her body even tighter to his…

"Garrett?"

He turned his head to look at her and knew instantly that had been a mistake. Desire glittered like hard diamonds in her eyes. He recognized it, because the same thing was happening to him. He felt it. His whole damn body was on fire, and he couldn't seem to fight it. More, he didn't want to.

He hadn't asked for this. Hadn't expected it. Didn't need it, God knew. But the plain truth was he wanted Alex so badly he could hardly breathe.

The worst part?

He couldn't have her.

He was working for her father. She was a princess. He was responsible for her safety. In the real world, a holiday romance was right up his alley. No strings. No questions. No complications. But *this* woman was nothing *but* complications. If he started something with Alex, regret would be waiting in the wings.

All good reasons for avoiding this situation. For brushing her off and steering this damn boat back to Decker's yard as fast as possible. For dropping her at her hotel and keeping an eye on her from a distance.

And not one of those reasons meant a damn thing in the face of the clawing need shredding his insides.

"Not a good idea, Alex," he managed to say.

"Why ever not?" She smiled and the brilliance of it was blinding. She leaned in closer and he could smell the soft, flowery scent of her shampoo.

Her question reverberated in his mind. *Why not?* He couldn't give her any of the reasons he had for keeping his hands to himself. So what the hell was he supposed to say?

That he was actually a monk? That he didn't find her the least bit attractive? She wouldn't buy either of those.

"It's a beautiful day," she said, pressing her body along his on the bench seat. "We're both on holiday—" She stopped suddenly and looked at him. "Unless you're involved with someone already and—"

"No." One word, forced through clenched teeth. He took a breath. "If I were, I wouldn't be here with you."

"Good. Then Garrett…kiss me again."

He ground his teeth in a last ditch effort to hang on to his rampaging desires, or at least his professionalism. Then her scent came to him again on a soft wind and he knew he was lost. Maybe he'd *been* lost since the moment he met her.

Alex the princess might be easy enough to ignore, but Alex the woman was an entirely different story.

He grabbed her, pulled her onto his lap as he moved out from under the steering wheel and looked down into her eyes. "This isn't a good idea."

"I think it's a brilliant idea," she countered with a smile, then lifted her face to his.

Her eyes were bright, her mouth so close he could almost taste it and her hair flew about them like a blond cloud, drawing him in. He didn't need any more encouragement. Right or wrong, this was inevitable.

He took what she offered, what he needed more than

he'd like to admit. He'd curse himself later for surrendering. For now, there was Alex, a soft sea breeze and the gentle lap of water against the hull of the boat. They were alone and damned if he'd waste another minute.

Six

His mouth came down on hers and the first taste of her sent Garrett over the edge. The kiss they'd shared at Disneyland had haunted him until he had damn near convinced himself that no kiss could be as good as he remembered it.

He was wrong.

It was better.

He knew the contours of her mouth now, how her body folded into him, the sigh of her breath on his cheek. She wrapped her arms around his neck and pressed herself more tightly to him. Her hands swept up into his hair, and each touch of her fingers was like lightning through his bloodstream.

He parted her lips with his tongue and she met him eagerly, stroking, tasting, exploring. Mouths fused, breaths mingling, hearts hammering in time, they came together with a desperate need that charged the air around them.

Garrett set his hands at her hips and lifted her up, shifting her around until she was straddling him, her pelvis pressed to his hard, aching groin. It wasn't enough, but it was a start. She groaned into his mouth as his hips arched up against her.

Alex moved with him, rocking her body against his, as demanding as he felt. She slanted her head, giving as well as taking, tangling her tongue with his, losing herself in the heat that seemed to be searing both of them.

His hands swept up, beneath the hem of that red shirt that had been making him crazy all morning. He skimmed his fingers across her skin until he could cup her lace-covered breasts in his palms. Then he swept his thumb back and forth across her erect nipples until she was twisting and writhing against him, grinding her hips against his.

Her kiss grew hungrier, more desperate.

He knew the feeling.

Her moans enflamed him. Her touch, the scrape of her short, neat fingernails over the back of his neck, felt like accelerant thrown onto a bonfire. He was being engulfed and he welcomed it.

It was as if everything in his life had come down to this moment with her. As if his hands had always ached for the touch of her. His body hard and ready, all he wanted was to peel her out of her white slacks and panties and bury himself inside her.

The ocean air slid around them like a cool caress, keeping the heat at bay and adding new sensations to the mix. Hair rippled, clothing was tugged as if even nature wanted them together in the most basic way.

"You're killin' me," he muttered, tearing his mouth from hers long enough to drag in a deep breath of the salt-stained air.

"No," she said with a sigh and a grin as she licked her lips. "Not interested in killing you at all, Garrett."

He returned that smile, and slowly lifted the hem of her shirt, baring her abdomen and more to his gaze. When her lace-covered breasts were revealed, he reached behind her, unhooked her bra with a flick of his fingers then lifted the lacy cups for his first good look at her breasts.

Round and full, with dark pink, pebbled nipples, they made his mouth water. He lifted his gaze to hers and saw passion glazing her eyes. She licked her bottom lip, drew a shallow breath and leaned into him.

"Taste me," she whispered.

And it would have taken a stronger man than Garrett to turn down that offer. He bent his head and took first one nipple, then the other into his mouth. Moving back and forth between them, he licked and nibbled at her sensitive skin until she was a jangle of need, practically vibrating against him.

Finally, he suckled at her left breast while tugging at the nipple of her right with his fingers. His tongue traced damp circles around her areola and his mouth worked at her, sucking and pulling, drawing as much of her as he could into him.

"Garrett, yes," she whispered, holding his head to her, as if afraid he might stop.

But he had no intention of stopping. Now that they had crossed the barrier keeping them apart, nothing would keep him from having her completely.

"That feels so good." She was breathless, her body moving of its own accord, looking for the release she needed.

And as she moved on him, his groin tightened to the point of real pain and he wouldn't change anything. He dropped one hand to the juncture of her thighs and through the material of her white slacks, he felt her heat. Felt the dampness gathering there at her core.

He rubbed her, pressing hard against the nub of sensation he knew would be aching as he ached. She groaned again, louder this time, and moved restlessly on him. Dropping her hands to the snap and zipper, she undid them, giving him a view of the pale, ivory lace panties she wore before going up on her knees on the bench seat.

Garrett released her nipple, looked up into her eyes and lost himself in their passion-filled depths. He lifted one hand and deliberately, slowly dipped his fingers beneath the elastic band of her panties. She took a breath, let her head fall back and tensed, waiting for his first touch.

She looked like a pagan goddess.

Breasts bared to the sun, face lifted to the sky, hair flying in the wind and her center, open and waiting. He was rocked right down to his soul. She was magnificent. And the need clamoring inside him whipped into a churning frenzy.

He cupped her heat with his palm and was rewarded by a soft sigh of pleasure that slid from her elegant throat. Garrett's hand moved lower, his fingers reaching. She moved with him, giving him easier access. Her hands dropped to his shoulders to steady herself and when his thumb stroked over that one bud of passion, she jolted and gasped in a breath.

"Garrett…Garrett…" It was both plea and temptation.

He watched her, gaze fixed on her expressive face as he dipped first one finger, then two, inside her damp heat. He worked her body, making her rock and twist as she climbed that ladder of need to the climax that was waiting for her. His thumb moved over that nub again and again until she was practically whimpering. Her fingers dug into his shoulders, her sighs came fast and furious.

He stroked her, inside and out, until her body was bowed with building tension, until she was so blindly wrapped up in her own need, he, too, felt the gathering storm. When the first shocking jolt of release hit her, Garrett steadied her with one hand while with the other he pushed her higher, and higher, demanding more, always more.

"I can't," she whispered brokenly. "No more..."

"There's always more," he promised and then delivered—another orgasm, crashing down on her right after the first.

She wobbled on unsteady knees and finally dropped to his lap. Only then did she open her eyes and look into his. Only then did she lean forward and kiss him with a long, slow passion that left him as breathless as she felt.

Never before had he taken so much pleasure from his partner's climax. Never before had he been willing to put his own needs on hold for the simple joy of watching a woman shatter in his arms.

Dragging his hand free of her body, he reached up and smoothed her tangled hair back from her face. Then he cupped her cheek and drew her in close. He kissed her then, relishing the slow slide of her tongue against his.

Alex's mind splintered under the assault of too many sensations at once. His hands, his mouth, his breath. He was everything. The center of the universe, and she was left spinning wildly in his orbit. This moment, this touch, this kiss, was everything.

And in the aftermath of two amazing orgasms, it was all she could do to breathe.

She had thought she knew what it was to kiss Garrett. Truthfully, though, she'd had no idea. This was so much *more* than she had experienced before, there was no way she could have been prepared for what she would feel when it was more than a kiss. When his touch lit up her insides like the firework-lit skies over the palace on Cadria's Coronation Day.

Alex stared into his blue eyes, suddenly as dark and mysteriously hypnotic as the deepest seas, and tried to gather up the frayed threads of her mind. A useless endeavor.

Her brain had simply shut down. Her body was in charge now and all she knew was that she needed him. Needed to feel his skin against hers. Though she was still trembling with the reaction of her last orgasm, she wanted more. She wanted his body locked inside hers.

She traced her fingertips across his cheek, smiled and whispered, "That was amazing. But we're not finished… are we?"

"Not by a long shot," he told her before he gave her a quick, hard kiss that promised so much more.

"Thank heaven," she answered and dropped her hands to the hem of his shirt. As she went to tug it up, though, a deep, throaty noise intruded. A noise that was getting closer. They both turned to see the speedboat, racing toward them again.

Instantly, Alex pulled her shirt down, fastened her bra and quickly did up her pants. The other boat was too far away still for anyone to get a glimpse of bare skin, but the intimacy of the moment had been shattered anyway, and she didn't want to risk a stranger getting a peek at her.

Garrett's gaze narrowed on the approaching craft and his mouth firmed into a grim line. In seconds, he went from ravaging lover to alert protector. He lifted her off his lap, slid behind the wheel of the boat and fired up the engine. The throaty roar pulsed out around them and still, the racing boat's motor screamed loud enough that Alex wanted to cover her ears.

They watched as the speedboat came closer, its hull bouncing and crashing over the surface of the water. A huge spray of water fantailed in its wake as the driver swung in their direction.

"What's he doing?" Alex shouted.

"I don't know," Garrett called out, focus locked on the fast-approaching watercraft.

The boat was close enough now that Alex could see a couple up near the front of the boat and a child standing alone in the back. She whipped her head around, but saw no one else nearby. Just the far away surfers and the jet boat coming ever closer.

"Guy's an idiot," Garrett told her as the boat swung into a sharp turn. "If he doesn't throttle back, someone's going to—"

Before he could finish the sentence, the child flew off the back of the boat, hit the water hard and promptly sank. The boat kept going, the two other people on board apparently unaware they had lost the child.

"Oh, my God!" Alex stood up, frantically waving both arms at the driver to get his attention, but she went unnoticed. "The boy! He hasn't surfaced!"

Garrett shut off the engine, yanked his shirt over his head and tossed it to the deck then shouted, "Stay on the boat!" before he dove into the water.

His body knifed below the surface so cleanly he hardly made a splash. Terrified, Alex watched as he swam with swift, sure strokes, tanned arms flashing in and out of the water as he headed for the spot where the boy had gone under.

Alex's stomach jumped with nerves. With outright fear. She threw a glance at the jet boat, still flying across the water then looked back to where Garrett was swimming purposefully toward the child in trouble. She felt helpless. Useless. She had to *do* something.

Sliding behind the wheel, she fired up the engine and carefully eased the throttle forward, inching the boat closer to Garrett. She'd never driven a boat before and the power at her hands terrified her. One wrong move and she could endanger both Garrett and the child. Too much gas, she could run over them—if she didn't hit them outright. And there was the damage the propellers below the surface could do.

Tension gripping her, Alex's hands fisted on the steering wheel as she fought her own fears and her sense of dread for both the boy and Garrett. She kept her gaze locked on Garrett's sleek figure slicing through the water. Where was the boy? Why hadn't he come up? How could Garrett find him?

Fear ratcheted up another notch or two inside her as she inched ever closer. She risked another glance around; she was still alone out here. The jet boat hadn't returned.

"Do you see him?" she shouted.

Garrett shook his head, water spraying from the ends of his hair just before he suddenly dived deep, disappearing beneath the water entirely.

Alex cut the engine and stood up, watching the ever-churning water, hoping, waiting. What felt like *hours* ticked past.

"Come on, Garrett," she chanted, studying the water, looking for any sign of him. "Come back up. Come on!"

How could he hold his breath that long? What should she do? If she jumped in as well, would she make it that much more dangerous? One more person flailing about? She wasn't a strong swimmer anyway.

She heard a roar of sound and turned her head to see the jet boat hurtling toward them. If they didn't slow down...

"Stop!" Waving her arms and jumping up and down like a crazy woman, Alex screamed and shouted to get their attention. Idiots. Complete idiots. Didn't they realize that they could run over both Garrett and the child they must have finally realized was missing?

The boat slowed and when the engine cut off, the silence was deafening.

"Tommy!" The woman yelled as the man on board dived off the stern of his boat. Hanging over the railing, the woman was oblivious to Alex's presence, her focus concentrated solely on the dark water and what might be happening below.

Alex felt the same.

She didn't know how long Garrett had been underwater. She'd lost track of time. Couldn't think. Could hardly breathe. Dimly, she was aware that prayers were whipping through her mind at a furious rate and she hoped that someone upstairs was listening.

Apparently, they were. *"There!"*

Alex pointed at the shadow of movement in the dark water as it headed toward the surface. The woman on the boat behind her was still screaming and wailing. Alex hardly heard her.

Garrett shot out of the water, shaking his hair back from his face. In his arms, a boy of no more than five or six lay limply, eyes closed. A moment later, the man from the jet boat popped up beside Garrett and tried to take the boy.

Garrett ignored him and swam toward the jet boat. Alex followed his progress, her gaze locked on him and on the pale, young face he towed toward safety.

"Oh, God. Oh, God." The woman was babbling now,

tears streaming down her face, voice breaking on every word. "Is he breathing? Is he breathing?"

Garrett laid the boy on the cut out steps at the back of the boat and tipped the child's head back. While Alex watched, Garrett blew into the boy's mouth once. Twice. The waiting was the worst part. The quiet, but for the water continually slapping the hull and the now quiet weeping from the woman who had to be the boy's mother.

Again, Garrett breathed air into the boy's lungs and this time, there was a reaction.

Coughing, sputtering, retching what seemed a gallon of sea water, the little boy arched up off the deck of the boat, opened his eyes and cried, "Mommy!"

Instantly, the woman was on her knees, gathering her son to her chest. Rocking him, holding him, murmuring words only he could hear between the sobs racking her.

Tears streaked down Alex's cheeks, too, as she watched the man in the water grab Garrett and give him a hard hug. "Thanks, man. Seriously, thank you. I don't know what— If you hadn't been here—"

Garrett's gaze drifted to Alex and she felt his fury and relief as surely as she felt her own. But mixed in with those churning emotions, pride in what Garrett had done swelled inside her. He'd saved that child. If not for him, the boy would never have been recovered. His parents might have spent hours looking, wondering exactly where the boy had fallen in, having no idea where to search for him.

"Glad I could help," Garrett said tightly. "Next time slow down. And give that kid a life vest when you're on a damn boat."

"Right. Right." The man swiped one hand across his face, looked up at his family and Alex saw him pale at the realization of what might have happened.

"Yeah," he said. "I will. I swear it."

"Thank you," the woman said, lifting her head long enough to look first at Garrett and then at Alex. "Thank you so much. I don't know what else to say—"

She broke off, her gaze narrowing as she stared at Alex, a question in her eyes. "Aren't you…"

A knot of panic exploded in Alex's stomach. Would this woman recognize her? Say something?

"You'd better get him to a doctor," Garrett blurted. "Have him checked out."

"Yes," the woman said, tearing her gaze away from Alex long enough to nod, then stare down at her son again. "Good idea. Mike?"

"Coming," the man said, pushing himself out of the water and onto the boat. "Thanks again. It's not enough but it's all I can say."

Relieved that not only the boy was safe, but her secret as well, Alex watched Garrett swim toward her. She paid no attention when the speedboat owners fired up their powerful engine and took off—at a slower pace than they had been going previously. She was just glad to see them gone. Of course she was happy the child had survived. Happy that Garrett had been able to save him. But she was also grateful that her identity was still a secret. What were the odds, she wondered, of being in the middle of an ocean with a child near drowning and that boy's mother recognizing her?

She shoved those thoughts away as Garrett braced his hands on the edge of the boat and hoisted himself inside. Then he just sat there, holding his head in his hands. Alex sat down beside him, uncaring about the water sluicing off his clothes, soaking into hers.

Alex wrapped her arms around him and leaned her head on his shoulder.

"You were wonderful," she said softly.

"I was lucky," he corrected, lifting his head to look at her. "Saw a flash of the kid's white T-shirt and made a blind grab for him."

"You saved him," Alex said, cupping his cheek in her palm. "You were wonderful, Garrett."

A slow smile curved his mouth. "If you say so."

She smiled too. "I do."

"I learned a long time ago—never argue with a beautiful woman." He caught her hand in his, squeezed it briefly then leaned in to give her a fast kiss. "But, I think our boating trip is over."

Her heart tumbled in her chest. She didn't want the day to end. It had been filled with emotional ups and downs and moments of sheer terror. A boy's life had been saved and her own life had taken a wild turn in a direction she hadn't expected.

Alex looked at Garrett and couldn't even imagine *not* being with him. She'd known him only two days and he had touched her more deeply than anyone she had ever known. He was strong and capable and funny. He kissed her and her body exploded with need. He caressed her and the world fell away. She had never felt more alive than she did when she was with Garrett.

So no, she didn't want this day to end because every day that passed put her one day closer to leaving—and never seeing him again.

"Hey," he asked, brow furrowing, "what is it? What's wrong?"

"Nothing," she said. "It's nothing. I just…didn't want today to be over, I suppose."

He brushed a kiss across her mouth and eased back. "Day's not over, Alex. Just the boat ride."

"Really?"

"Really. Dress codes in five-star restaurants are a

lot looser in California than anywhere else, but…" He slapped one hand against his jeans and looked ruefully at his sodden boots. "I think they'll draw the line at soaking wet. I need to change clothes before I take you to dinner."

What he was saying made sense, but the look in his eyes told a different story. It was as if in saving the child, he'd closed a part of himself off from her, and Alex wanted to know why. He was pulling back, even sitting here beside him. She could feel a wall going up between them and wasn't sure what to do about it.

So for now, she let it go and gave him the answer she knew he was expecting.

"In that case," she told him, "we'd better get going."

Seven

The King Security company building was quiet. Halls were dark, phones silent and Garrett appreciated the peace. The light on his desk shone like a beam of sunlight in the darkness as he added his signature to a stack of papers Griffin had already signed in his absence.

The puddle of light from his desk lamp was bright and golden and threw the rest of the room into deep shadow. But Garrett didn't need light to find his way around. This place had pretty much been his life for the past ten years. He and Griffin had adjoining offices with a shared bathroom complete with shower separating them. There were plenty of times they had to leave fast for a job and having a shower and a change of clothes around came in damn handy.

There were bookcases on two of the walls and floor-to-ceiling windows overlooking the ocean on another. Family photographs and paintings hung on the remaining wall, and plush leather furniture completed the room. There was a fireplace, wet bar and a long couch comfortable enough to have served as Garrett's bed more than once.

This was the company he and Griffin had built with a lot of hard work, tenacity and the strength of their reputation. He was proud of it and until recently, hadn't so much as taken a day off. Garrett King lived and breathed the job. At least he *had,* until Alex came into his life.

And just like that, she was at the forefront of his thoughts again.

Instantly, his mind turned back to the afternoon on Decker's boat. His body reached for the sense memory of Alex trembling against him, but his brain went somewhere else. To the child falling into the water and nearly drowning. To Garrett's split-second decision to leave Alex alone and unprotected while he saved the child.

He couldn't have done it differently and he knew that, but still the decision haunted him. She had been alone. What if it had all been a setup? Some cleverly disguised assassination or kidnapping attempt on a crown princess? Sure, chances were slim, but they were *there.* The boy could have been a champion swimmer, doing exactly what he had been paid to do.

Absurd? he asked himself. Maybe. Paranoid? Absolutely. But stranger things had happened, and he'd been around to see a lot of them. Gritting his teeth, Garrett silently fumed at his complete lack of professionalism. He'd saved the boy but risked Alex and that was not acceptable.

He could still feel the slide of her skin beneath his fingers. Hear her whispered cries and the catch in her breath as her climax took her. His body went hard and tight as stone and he told himself the pain was only what he deserved.

Never should have let any of it happen, he told himself.

Hell, he knew better. Years ago, he'd learned the hard way that putting your own wants before the job was a dangerous practice that could end up costing lives.

Garrett threw the pen and swiped one arm across his desk, sending the stack of papers flying like a swarm of paper airplanes. Releasing his temper hadn't helped, though, and he pushed back from his desk, swiping one hand across his face. His eyeballs felt like sand-crusted rocks. He couldn't sleep for dreams of Alex.

That was why he was here, in the middle of the night. He had hoped that focusing his mind on work would keep thoughts of Alex at bay. So far he'd been there for two hours and it wasn't working.

Instead his brain insisted on replaying that scene in the boat over and over again. Those few, stolen, amazing moments that even now, he couldn't really regret. How the hell could he?

He had tried to tell himself that Alex was no different than any other celebrity or royal needing protection. That being with her didn't really mean a damn thing. But then she would laugh and his calm reason flew out the window.

The woman had a hell of a laugh.

It was just part of what he'd noticed about Alex at Disneyland. What set her apart from every other female Garrett had ever known.

She threw herself into life—she held nothing back. Even there in his arms, she had been open and vulnerable, offering him everything. It was damn sexy to watch, and every minute with her was a kind of enjoyable misery. His body was so tight and hard, he could hardly walk. He felt like a damn teenager again. No woman had ever affected him like this. Which was a big problem. She wasn't his. Not even temporarily.

She was a damn princess, and he was lying to her every

minute he was around her. She thought she was free and on her own, and he was being paid by her father to look out for her.

How much deeper was this hole he was in going to get?

Shaking his head, Garrett bent to scoop up the fallen papers and shuffle them back into some kind of order. Griffin had been right when he had ragged on Garrett for being practically monklike for months. Garrett had long ago burned out on women who were more interested in what being seen with a King could do for them than they were in him. And frankly, the women he knew were all the damn same. They all talked about the same things, thought the same way and, in general, bored the hell out of him.

Not Alex.

Nothing about her was ordinary. Or boring.

He never should have called the king. Never should have agreed to this bodyguard gig. Hell, he never should have gone to Disneyland.

Yeah, he told himself wryly. It was all Jackson's fault. If he'd never gone with his cousin and his family, if he'd never met Alex at all…he didn't like the thought of that, either.

"Son of a bitch." He tossed the papers to his desktop and glared at them hard enough to start a fire.

"Problem?"

Garrett snapped a look at the open doorway where his twin stood, one shoulder braced against the doorjamb. The shadows were so thick, he couldn't see Griffin's face, but the voice was unmistakable.

"What're you doing here in the middle of the night?" Garrett leaned back in his black leather chair and folded his hands atop his flat abdomen.

"Funny," Griffin said, pushing away from the doorway

to wander into his brother's office, "I was going to ask you the same thing." He dropped into one of the visitor's chairs opposite Garrett. "Was headed home from Amber's place and imagine my surprise when I spotted a single light on in the office. I figured it was either you or a really stupid burglar."

Garrett looked at his twin. His tuxedo was wrinkled, the collar of his shirt opened halfway down his chest and the undone bow tie was hanging down on both sides of his neck. Apparently at least *one* of them had had a good night.

"How is Amber?"

Griffin snorted and shoved one hand through his hair. "Still talking about getting that modeling job in Paris. I heard all about her packing tips, what she'll be wearing in the runway show and what kind of exfoliant will leave her skin—and I quote here—'shimmery.'"

He had to laugh. Shaking his head, he studied his brother and asked, "Why do you insist on dating women who don't have two active brain cells?"

"There are…compensations," Griffin said with a grin. "Besides, you date women who can walk and talk at the same time and you don't look happy."

"Yeah, well." What the hell could he say? He wasn't happy. Things with Alex were more complicated than ever.

He was tangled up in knots of hunger and frustration. Torn by his sense of duty and responsibility. For two days, he'd fought his every urge and instinct. All he wanted to do was get Alex naked and have her to himself for a few hours. Or weeks.

Instead, he'd made damn sure that the scene in the boat or anything remotely like it, hadn't happened again. For those few moments with Alex, Garrett had allowed himself to forget who and what she was. To put aside the reality of the situation. He'd indulged himself—putting her in a potentially dangerous situation—and now he was paying for it.

Every cell in his body was aching for her. He closed his eyes to sleep and he saw her. He caught her scent in his car, on his clothes. He was being haunted, damn it, and there didn't seem to be a thing he could do about it.

Disgusted, he said, "I'm happy."

"Yeah, I'm convinced." Griffin scowled at him.

He was really not in the mood to listen to his twin. He didn't want to hear about how he should let go of the past. Stop blaming himself for what had happened so long ago. He didn't want to talk. Period.

"Go away," he said, snatching up his pen again and refocusing on the papers in an attempt to get Griffin moving. Of course, it didn't work.

"Princess giving you problems?"

Garrett's gaze snapped to his twin's.

"Whoa. Quite the reaction." Griffin's eyebrows lifted. "So she's getting to you, huh?"

He dropped the pen, scraped both hands across his face and then shoved them through his hair. When that didn't ease his tension, he pushed out of his chair and stalked to the window overlooking the ocean. The moon was out, shining down on the water, making its surface look diamond studded. It was a scene that had soothed him many times over the years. Now, all it did was remind him of Alex. Of being on that boat in the sunshine. Of holding her while she—

"She's not getting to me. Everything's fine. Leave it alone, Griff."

"I don't think so." His twin stood up and walked to join him at the window. "What's going on, Garrett?"

"Nothing. Absolutely *nothing*. That's the problem."

Griffin studied him for a long minute or two and even in the shadowy light, Garrett saw amusement flicker in his twin's eyes. "You've got it bad, don't you?"

"You don't know what you're talking about."

"Right. Everything's great with you. That's why you're here. In the middle of the night, sitting alone in the dark."

"My desk light's on."

"Not the point."

"What *is* the point, Griffin?"

His twin gave him a half smile. "The point is, the mighty Garrett King is falling for a princess."

"You're out of your mind."

"Sure I am."

"She's a job. Her father hired us, remember?"

"Uh-huh."

"She's a princess. And God knows I'm no prince."

"Rich as one," Griffin pointed out helpfully.

"It's not enough and you know it." He shook his head. "Royalty hangs with royalty. Period."

"Not lately." When Garrett glared at him, Griffin shrugged. "I'm just sayin'…

He shifted his gaze away from his twin and stared unseeing at the ocean. Alex's face swam into his mind and as much as he tried to ignore it, she wouldn't go away. He was getting in too deep here and he knew it. But damned if he could see a way out.

"She's a job," he repeated, and which of them he was trying harder to convince, Garrett wasn't sure.

"Sure she is." Griffin slapped him on the shoulder. "Look, making yourself nuts over this just isn't worth it, Garrett. Why not just tell her the truth? Tell her who you are, that you're working for her father."

He'd thought about it. But confessing all wouldn't solve

anything. He'd still want her. And he still wouldn't be able to have her. And as a bonus, she'd be hurt.

"Can't do that."

"Fine, then let me take over," Griffin said.

Garrett just stared at him. "What?"

"Wouldn't be the first time we twin-switched somebody."

"You can't be serious," Garrett said with a snort of laughter.

"Why not? If she's just a job, I'll show up as you, spend some time with her…"

"Stay the hell away from her, Griffin."

His twin grinned. "So I'm right. She *does* mean something to you."

Blowing out a breath, Garrett frowned and turned his face back to the window. His own reflection stared back at him.

"Yeah, guess she does," he murmured, talking to his brother but somehow hoping to reassure the man in the glass as well. "Damned if I know what, though. But in another week or so she'll be gone. Problem solved."

"You think so?"

"I know it." All he had to do was find a way to keep his hands off her. Then she'd be back behind palace doors and his life would go back to normal. If the man in the glass didn't look reassured at all, Garrett ignored it.

Glancing at his twin, he deliberately changed the subject. "As long as you're here, bring me up to speed on what's going on with the business."

"Garrett…"

"Drop it, Griff," he said tightly. "Just, drop it."

"The most stubborn son of a—fine. Okay then, we've got a new client." Griffin moved back to the chair and sat down, stretching out his legs and crossing them at the ankle. "He's opening a luxury resort in Georgia and apparently he's having trouble with some local protestors."

"What're they protesting?"

Griffin snorted. "He's building a golf course and apparently threatening the home ground of the three-legged-gnat-catcher-water-beast-frog or some damn thing. Anyway, to protect the insects, they're threatening our client, and he wants to hire us to protect his family."

"It's a weird world, brother," Garrett muttered. "Protect the gnats by killing people."

"You got that right. Still, upside is, the weirdness is good for business. Anyway…"

Garrett nodded and listened while his brother outlined his plans for their latest client. This was better. Work. Something definable. Something he could count on. All he had to do was keep his focus centered. Remember who he was and why it was so important to keep a hard demarcation line between him and Alex.

He took a seat behind his desk, picked up the pen and began making notes. King Security was his reality.

Not a runaway princess looking for a white knight.

Three days.

It had been three days since they were together on that boat. Three days since Garrett had touched her in any but the most impersonal way. Three days that Alex had spent in a constant state of turmoil, waiting for it all to happen again and then being crushed when *nothing* happened.

Which was making her insane.

"Honestly," she demanded out loud of the empty room, "what is he waiting for?"

She knew he wanted her as much as she did him. When they were together, she felt the tension rippling off him in waves. So *why* was he working so hard at keeping her at arm's length? And why was she allowing it? For heaven's sake, this wasn't the nineteenth century. If she wanted him, she should go after him. No subtlety. No more waiting. He was determined to ignore what was between them, and she was just as determined that he be unable to.

Time was running out for her, Alex thought grimly. Soon enough, she would be on a plane headed back to Cadria and all of this would be nothing but a memory. And damn it, if memories were all that was going to be left of her, then she wanted as many of them as she could make.

With that thought firmly in mind, she checked her mirror and gave herself an objective once-over. Garrett had had some business to take care of that morning and so she'd had a couple of hours to herself and hadn't wasted them. A cab had taken her to the nearest mall where she had shopped until her feet gave out.

It had been good, walking through the Bella Terra mall, just another woman shopping. The freedom she felt was still thrilling, and she didn't know how she would get used to being under the palace microscope once her bit of freedom had ended. Being just one of a crowd was so liberating. She'd laughed with salesgirls, had a hamburger in the food court and then spent a lovely hour in a bookstore.

In fact, it would have been a perfect morning but for the fact that she'd had the oddest sensation that she was being watched. Ridiculous really and probably her own nerves rattling around inside her. No one here knew who she was so why would anyone be interested in what she was doing? She simply wasn't totally accustomed to being alone, that was all. Since leaving her guards behind her, she had been with Garrett almost every moment. Of course she would feel a touch uncomfortable. But it meant nothing.

Brushing off those thoughts, she returned to studying her reflection with a critical eye.

Hair good, makeup perfect and the slinky black dress she'd purchased just that morning clung to her like a second skin. The neckline was deep, displaying cleavage that should surely catch Garrett's eye. And the hemline was just barely legal. Paired with a pair of four-inch black heels, she looked, if she had to say so herself, hot.

Which was her intention, after all.

Her insides swirled with anticipation as she imagined the look on Garrett's face when he saw her. "Let him try to ignore me *now*."

A smile curved her mouth as she let her mind wander to all sorts of interesting places. Damp heat settled at her core and a throbbing ache beat in time with her pulse. She needed him as she had never needed anyone before. And tonight, she was going to make sure he knew it.

An extremely vivid memory rose up in her mind. In a flash, she recalled just how it felt to have Garrett kissing her, touching her. Showering her body with the kinds of sensations she'd never known before. And she wanted it again, blast it.

"What's missing in this holiday romance," she told her reflection sternly, "is *romance*."

Her time here was almost over. She couldn't very well put off her return indefinitely. First of all, she wouldn't do that to her family. But secondly, even if she *tried,* her father would never stand for it. If she didn't go home soon, the king would have an army of investigators out searching for her and they *would* find her. Her father was nothing if not thorough.

Now that she considered it actually, she was a little surprised her father hadn't already sent a herd of search dogs after her. It wasn't like him to let her minirebellion stand.

Frowning at the girl in the mirror, Alex shifted her gaze to the telephone on the bedside table. Guilt gnawed at her as she thought about calling home. At least letting her mother know that she was safe. The problem was, reaching her mother wouldn't be easy. The queen didn't have an email account. And she refused to get a cell phone, despite the palace and the king's insistence, so Alex would have to go through the palace phone system. Then she would have to talk to who knew how many ladies-in-waiting, assistants and secretaries before finally reaching her mother.

And during that interminable wait, everyone she talked to could spill the beans to her father the king, and Alex was in no mood to hear another lecture on the evils of selfishness.

"No," she said, staring at the phone, "I'm sorry, Mother, but I'll be home soon enough."

Just thinking about home had Alex imagining the castle walls closing in around her. She took a deep breath and reminded herself that she was still free. Still on her own. She still had time to enjoy life in the real world. To enjoy her time with Garrett.

Garrett.

She frowned again and turned to the laptop computer sitting on the desk near the terrace. She still didn't know Garrett's last name. They'd never discussed it again after that first time when they had decided to keep their identities a mystery. But…she did know his *cousin's* last name.

Garrett had kept her so busy the past couple of days, she'd hardly had a moment to think about the possibilities that knowledge provided. Every day had been so filled with activities and rushing about that when he brought her back to the hotel at night, she was so exhausted she usually just fell into bed.

But tonight…

She chewed at her bottom lip and wondered. What if there was a reason Garrett hadn't made any further moves?

Maybe he had lied when he said he wasn't involved with someone. Maybe he had a *wife*. That thought jolted and rocked through her on an equal tide of disappointment and righteous indignation.

For the first time, she considered the fact that she actually had a *reason* for keeping her last name a secret. Perhaps Garrett did, too.

"Right, then," she told herself. "Time to find out more about Garrett."

Decision made, she walked quickly to the computer, booted it up and took a chance. She entered the name Garrett King in the search engine and hit Enter.

In seconds, her world tilted and her stomach dropped. The first listing read *King Security, Garrett and Griffin King*.

King Security?

She couldn't believe it. Mouth dry, heart pounding, she clicked on the link and watched as their website opened up. She clicked on the About Us tab and there he was.

Her Garrett.

Garrett King.

Security expert.

"Bloody hell."

Garrett waited outside the penthouse door. He shot his cuffs, smoothed the lapels of his tailored, navy blue suit and wondered what the hell was taking Alex so long. Damn, hadn't taken him much time to get used to her being painfully punctual. Now that she was taking a few seconds to open the door, he was both bothered and worried.

Was she safe?

He knocked again and the door flew open. Alex was there and she looked...amazing.

The misery of the past couple of days gathered into a twist of knots in his gut. Just looking at her was pure, unadulterated torture. How the hell was he supposed to not touch her?

Garrett took a breath and reminded himself *again* of just what had happened the last time he'd allowed his dick to make his decisions for him. He had thrown professionalism aside in favor of his own wants and someone else had paid the price.

He'd be damned before he'd do the same damn thing again and have Alex paying for it.

When she just stared at him, he finally said, "You're so beautiful, you're dangerous."

She inclined her head in what he could only call a "regal" gesture. "Thank you." Grabbing her black bag from a nearby table, she hooked her arm through his and stepped out of the suite. "Shall we go?"

"Sure." Frowning to himself, Garrett felt the first stirrings of unease creep through him.

If he were out in the field, he'd be checking for snipers or some other bad guy sneaking up on him. It was just a feeling, but it had never let him down before.

Something was wrong.

Damian's was the hottest new restaurant on the coast. Designed to mimic the lush, noir atmosphere of the forties, the restaurant boasted a view of the ocean, a teakwood dance floor, linen-draped tables dusted with candlelight and the best seafood in California.

The place had struck a solid chord with the public— older people loved coming here to remember their youth and the younger crowd seemed to enjoy the romance and elegance of another era. It was easier to get a private audience with the pope than it was to land a reservation at

Damian's. Not a problem for Garrett, of course. It paid to be related to the owner.

A singer on stage, backed by a small orchestra working to evoke the feel of the big band era crooned about apple trees and lost loves. Dancers swayed to the music, bathed in spotlights that continually swept the floor.

Garrett wasn't surprised this place was a rousing success. Damian King was known for running restaurants that became legendary. At the moment, Damian was in Scotland, brokering a deal for a new "ghost" theme club to be opened in Edinburgh.

Jefferson King was happily living in Ireland. Garrett's brother Nash called London home and now Damian was in Scotland. He smiled to himself as he realized the Kings of California were slowly but surely starting to take over the world.

"It's lovely," Alex said and he turned to look at her.

Those were the first words she'd spoken to him since they'd left her hotel. She'd been polite, cool and completely shut off from him. The complete opposite of the Alex he had come to know over the last several days. There was no joy in her eyes, no easy smile and her spine was so straight, her shoulders so squared, it was as if she were tied to her chair.

"Yeah," he said warily. "Damian did a nice job of it. But then he always does."

"This isn't his only restaurant?"

"No, he's got a string of 'em up and down California."

"Interesting."

Okay, this was not right. She couldn't have made it plainer that something was chewing at her insides. He studied her and tried to figure out what the hell was going on. It was his *business,* after all, to be able to read people.

But for the first time since he'd known Alex, he didn't have a clue what was going on in her mind.

Her eyes were cool, dispassionate. Her luscious mouth was curved in a half smile that didn't reach her eyes. She was the epitome of the kind of sophisticated, aloof woman he usually avoided. Who was she and what had she done with Alex?

"Your cousin. That would be Damian *King?*"

"Yeah."

She nodded again, letting her gaze slide from his briefly. When she looked back at him again it was as if she was looking at a stranger.

That eerie-ass feeling he'd had earlier rose up inside him again. This whole night had been off from the jump. Something was up with Alex, and she wasn't even trying to hide it. He watched her. Waited. And had the distinct sensation that he wasn't going to like what was coming. She stroked her fingertips along the stem of the crystal water glass, and he was damn near hypnotized by the action.

A waitress approached and Garrett waved her away. Whatever was coming, he didn't want an audience for it. Keeping his gaze locked on the woman opposite him, he asked, "What's going on, Alex?"

"I was just wondering," she said, icicles dripping from her tone, "how many lies you've told me since the day we met."

A sinking sensation opened up in the pit of his stomach. A dark, yawning emptiness that spread throughout his system as the seconds ticked past.

"How long have you known?" she demanded quietly, her blue gaze frosty as it locked with his. "How long have you known who I am, Mr. *King?*"

The proverbial crap was about to hit the fan. He

shouldn't have been surprised. Alex was a smart woman. Sooner or later she was going to figure things out. Put two and two together and, any way you added it up, he was going to look like an ass.

No wonder everything had felt off to him tonight, Garrett thought grimly.

The woman sitting opposite him wasn't the Alex he knew.

This was Princess Alexis.

Eight

He didn't say anything.

Alex watched him, saw the flicker of an emotion dart across his eyes, but it came and went so quickly she couldn't identify it. Why wasn't he talking? Explaining? Because there was nothing he could say? Because if he tried to explain, it would only result in *more* lies?

The anger that had filled her since she had found his website spiked and roiled inside her. It had cost her every ounce of her self-control to keep what she was feeling locked within. She'd waited, half hoping that he would tell her the truth spontaneously. But then, why would he, when he was such a consummate liar?

King Security.

Alex felt like an idiot.

She'd believed everything.

Had *trusted* him, when all along, it had been nothing more than a game. He'd pretended to *like* her. Pretended to be attracted to her. When all along, he had known that she was a princess. God, she was a fool.

Garrett and his company had actually *been* to the palace. Had done work for her father. She hadn't recognized him because when he was in Cadria to provide security for the crown jewel celebration, Alex had avoided the whole situation. At the time, she and her father had been feuding over her involvement with the women's shelter. She'd been so furious with her father that she'd refused to have anything to do with the palace goings-on. Including, it seemed, meeting the security man brought in for the occasion.

If she had, she would have noticed Garrett. Looking at him even now, she could admit that he was most definitely a hard man to ignore. And if she'd met him then, she would have recognized him at Disneyland.

None of this would have happened. Her heart wouldn't be bruised, her feelings wouldn't be battered and she wouldn't now be wrapped in what felt like an icy blanket from head to toe.

She never would have found something with him that she could convince herself was real. She never would have believed that she, too, had discovered the same kind of magic her mother had found at the famous amusement park.

Instead she was left feeling the fool and staring into the eyes of a man she had thought she knew.

"How long?" she demanded, keeping her voice low enough that no one but him could hear her.

The strains of the music rose up and swelled around them, and the irony of the slow, romantic sound wasn't lost on her. She had hoped for so much from tonight. She'd wanted to seduce Garrett. Now all she could hope for was that she wouldn't get angry enough to cry.

She *hated* crying when she was furious.

Tilting her head to one side, she watched him. "Did you know at Disneyland?"

"Not right away," he admitted, and the iron bands around her chest tightened another inch or so until every breath was a minor victory.

That statement told her that at least part of what she had thought of as a magical day had been colored with lies.

Betrayal slapped at her. Was it before he'd kissed her in the dark during the pirate ride? While they laughed with his nieces on the carousel?

She looked into his blue eyes and searched for the man who had been with her on his cousin's boat a few days ago. The man who had touched her, shown her just how amazing two people could be together. But Alex didn't see him. Instead, she saw a cool-eyed professional, already pulling back from her. A part of her wondered how he could turn his emotions on and off so easily. Because right at that moment, she'd like nothing better than to be able to do the same.

"I didn't know you at first," he was saying. "Not until you and Molly were standing at the castle, talking about being a princess."

She nodded, swallowed hard and said, "So that's why you insisted on taking me home that night."

"Partly," he admitted.

She laughed shortly, the sound scraping against her throat. "Partly. It wasn't about me that night, Garrett. Not *me,* Alex. It was about protecting a princess. And you've been with me every day since for the same reason, haven't you?"

Scraping one hand across the back of his neck, he said, "I called your father that first night."

"Oh, God…" Just when she thought the icy cold enveloping her couldn't get worse…it did.

"I told him where you were. That you were alone and that I was…concerned."

"You had no right."

"I had a responsibility."

"To *whom?*" she demanded.

"To myself," he snapped. "I couldn't walk away leaving you unprotected once I knew who you really were."

"No one asked for your help."

"Your father did."

She shook her head, not wanting to hear any more. But she knew that was a futile hope.

"That's wonderful. Really. Your responsibility. Your decision. Your phone call." She narrowed her gaze on him. "But *my* life. This was never about you, Garrett. This was about me. What I wanted. And it never mattered, did it? Not to you. Not to anyone."

"Alex—"

She looked around the restaurant as if searching for an exit. But all she saw were couples sitting at tables, laughing, talking, easy with each other. They were enjoying the restaurant, the music, the romance of the place, and Alex suddenly envied them all so much it choked her.

"I never intended to hurt you."

"How nice for you then," she said, looking back at him. "Because you haven't hurt me. You've enraged me."

"Now who's lying?"

That snapped her mouth shut and all she could do was glare at him. Yes, she was lying because she *was* hurt. Devastated, in fact, but damned if she would show him how much his lies had cut at her.

"There's more," he said.

"Of course there is."

"Like I said before, your father hired me to protect you."

His words sunk into her consciousness like a rock tossed to the bottom of a lake. The sense of betrayal she had felt before was *nothing* compared to this. Her mouth opened and closed a few times as she struggled to speak past the hard knot of something bitter lodged in her throat. Finally, though, she managed to blurt, "Yes, he's *paying* you to spend time with me."

Garrett huffed out a breath and glanced to each side of him before he spoke again and a small part of Alex's brain chided her for dismissing just how careful he was. For thinking that he was simply a cautious man. She remembered thinking not long after they met that he was acting a lot like one of the palace guards. Foolish of her not to realize just what that actually might mean.

Then she pushed those thoughts aside and concentrated solely on what he was saying.

"Your father hired me as a personal bodyguard. We were both worried about what might happen if you were on your own."

"Yes," she said tightly, amazed that she could form thoughts, let alone *words*. "Can't have Alex out and about behaving like an actual person. No, no. Can't have *that*."

"Damn it, Alex, you're deliberately misunderstanding."

"I don't think so," she snapped. "And you know? Maybe you and my father were right. Maybe poor Alex doesn't have a brain in her head. After all, she was foolish enough to think a handsome man wanted to know her better when, in reality, he was on her father's payroll." Her fingers clenched into useless fists. She wanted to throw something. To surrender to the temper frothing and boiling inside her. Unfortunately, her breeding and training had been too thorough. Duty and dignity ran through her veins along with the blood.

Circumspection was another watchword of the royal family and she was too steeped in its tradition to give rein to what she was feeling now. Still, she couldn't continue sitting across from him as if this were a date. She couldn't look at him now without feeling like a complete idiot. She couldn't watch his eyes, cool and dark, without remembering the heat and passion that had flared there so briefly.

At that thought, she gaped at him, horrified. "What about the boat? What happened there? Are you getting a bonus?"

"What?"

She leaned in toward him, pushing the flickering candle to one side. "Was that on the agenda? Show the princess a good time? Or did you just want bragging rights? Want to be able to tell your friends how you got a princess naked? Is that it?"

He leaned in, too, and the flare of the candle flame threw dancing patterns across his features. His eyes were more shadowed, his cheekbones more pronounced. "You know damn well that's not true."

"Do I?" she countered. "Do I really? I know! I should trust you on this because you've been so honest with me from the first, I suppose."

"You kept secrets, too," he argued.

That stopped her for a second. But only a second. "I did, but I wasn't *spying* on you."

"I'm not a damn spy!" His voice pitched a little too loud just as the song ended and several people turned to look. He glared them away before staring back at her. "I told your father I wouldn't be an informer, and I haven't been."

"Again," she said coolly, "with your sterling reputation, I should just take your word?"

His mouth worked furiously as though he were fighting an inner battle to keep his temper in check and angry words from spilling free. Well, she knew just how he felt.

Finally, he managed to say, "You're angry, I get it."

"Oh, I'm well beyond angry, Mr. King," she snapped and stood up. "Fury is a good word and still it doesn't capture exactly what I'm feeling. But thankfully, neither of us has to suffer the other's presence any further."

"Where do you think you're going?" he asked, standing up to look down at her.

Her body lit up inside and Alex silently cursed her response to him. What was it about this man that he could get to her even when she was more furious than she had ever been in her *life?* That simply wasn't right. "Anywhere but here. This *is* a free country, isn't it?"

"Alex, don't do anything foolish just because you're mad."

"I'll do what I please, Garrett King, and I'll thank you to stay away from me." She turned to go, but he caught her arm and held on to her.

She glared down at his hand and then lifted her gaze to his. "You know, when we first met, I thought you were a hero. Now I know you're the villain in the piece."

The muscle in his jaw twitched, and she knew he was grinding his teeth into powder. Good to know that she wasn't the only one feeling as if the top of her head was about to blow off.

"I'm not a hero. Never claimed to be. But I'm not a damn villain, either, Alex. I'm just a man."

"Doing his *job,*" she finished for him and jerked her arm free of his grasp. "Yes, I know."

Head up, chin lifted in a defiant tilt, she headed for the bar. He was just a step or two behind her. "What're you doing?"

"I think I need a drink."

"Don't be an idiot. Come back to the table. We'll talk about this."

"Now I'm an idiot, am I?"

"I didn't *say* that," he muttered.

"Well, you're right on one score. I have *been* an idiot. But not any longer." She hissed in a breath. "I don't want to talk to you, Garrett. Go away."

"Not a chance," he whispered, close to her ear.

His deep voice rumbled along her spine and lifted goose bumps across her flesh. She so wanted to be unaffected by him. But it looked as though *that* wasn't going to happen anytime soon.

The worst part of all of this? Beyond the humiliation of her father going behind her back and the man she was... involved with selling her out to the palace?

She still wanted Garrett.

Mingled in with the anger and the hurt were the underlying threads of desire that still had her wrapped up in knots. How could she still want him, knowing what she did now?

Alex stalked into the bar and gave a quick glance around. There were a dozen or so tall tables with singles and couples gathered at them. A long, gleaming bar snaked around the room in a semicircle. Three bartenders in World War II military uniforms hurried back and forth filling drink orders. Mirrors behind the bar reflected the candlelight and the stony face of the man standing behind her.

The face that had haunted her dreams from the day they met. Their gazes locked in the mirror and Alex felt a jolt of something hot and wicked sizzle through her system in spite of everything.

Deliberately, she tore her gaze from his and walked to

the bar, sliding onto one of the black leather stools. She crossed her legs, laid her bag on the bar top and ordered a gin and tonic.

In the bar mirror, she watched Garrett take a seat a few stools down from her. Not far enough, she thought, but better than nothing. She was only surprised that he was giving her this small amount of space.

"Hello, gorgeous." A deep voice spoke up from just behind her and Alex lifted her gaze to the mirror.

A tall, blond man wearing a black suit and a wide smile stood watching her. "You are way too beautiful to be alone," he said and sat down without waiting for an invitation.

"Thank you, that's very kind." She saw Garrett's reaction from the corner of her eye and seeing him fume made her smile a welcome at the man beside her.

"An accent, too?" He slapped one hand to his heart in a dramatic gesture that had Alex smiling. "You're going to fuel my dreams for weeks."

"That's a lovely thing to say," she told him, though truthfully she thought he was a little on the ridiculous side. With his glib lines, and over-the-top reactions, he was nothing like Garrett with his quiet, deadly, sexy air. Ordinarily, in fact, she wouldn't have been the slightest bit interested in the blond. Still, she caught a glimpse of Garrett's face in the mirror and noted the abject fury on his features. So she leaned toward her new admirer and asked, "What's your name, love?"

"I'm Derek. Who're you?"

"Alexis," she said, "but you can call me Alex."

"You're no 'Alex,' babe," he said with a wink. "So Alexis it is."

In the other room, the music started up again and Derek stood, holding out one hand. "Dance?"

From the corner of her eye, Alex saw Garrett stand up as if he was going to try to stop her. So she quickly took Derek's hand and let him lead her to the floor.

Damn woman.

She was doing this on purpose. Letting that slick guy give her a lame line and then sweep her off to the dance floor. Well, fine, if that's what she wanted, she could have the plastic blond guy. But she wouldn't be alone with him. Garrett was still working for her father and damned if he was going to leave a woman like Alex to the likes of *that* guy.

He followed them into the other room and stood to one side as the blond pulled Alex into his arms and started moving to the music. Alex looked like a vision. That wild mane of blond hair, those heels that made her legs look ten miles long and where the hell had she gotten that dress, anyway? Didn't she know he could practically see her *ass?*

Alex laughed at something Blondie had to say and Garrett's teeth crushed together. He'd known from the start that his lies would eventually catch up with him. Maybe, he told himself, he should have listened to Griffin and confessed the truth to Alex himself. Then at least he would have had the chance to smooth things over with the telling.

But how much smoothing could he have done, realistically? She would still have been hurt. Still have been pissed. And he'd *still* end up standing here watching as some other guy made moves on her.

Moves, he told himself, that she wasn't deflecting.

Irritated beyond belief, Garrett stood like a statue, arms crossed over his chest, feet braced wide apart in a fighting stance. His gaze never left the couple as he watched Blondie ooze his way across the dance floor. Surely, Alex wasn't buying this guy's lines? Any minute now in fact, she'd probably step out of the dance and walk away.

Any minute.

Walking.

Damn it, Alex.

The music slid around the room and the singer's voice wrapped them all in a sensual web. His arms ached to hold her. His hands warmed at the thought of touching her again and his mouth craved the taste of her.

His eyes narrowed as Blondie steered Alex off the dance floor and out onto the dark balcony overlooking the ocean. While the music played and couples danced, Garrett moved through the crowd with a quiet intensity. Focused on his target, he was aware of his surroundings in a heightened way, but all he could think about was reaching Alex.

He stepped onto the polished wood balcony and heard the rush of the sea pushing into shore. Moonlight washed the whole scene in a silvery glow and the wind sweeping across the ocean was nearly icy. Voices came to him and he turned his head in response. That's when he spotted them, at the end of the deck, in a puddle of darkness that lay between the more-decorative-than-useful balcony lights.

Alex was facing the water, and Blondie was plastered up behind her, as close as he could get. Garrett's mind splintered a little and he actually *saw* red around the edges of his vision.

Then his eyes nearly popped from his head in an onslaught of pure fury. Blondie had one hand on Alex's ass and was giving it a rub—and Alex wasn't even trying to stop him.

What the hell?

It only took a few, long strides to carry him to Alex's

side, where he dropped one hand on Blondie's shoulder and squeezed. Blondie looked up, annoyed at the interruption, but annoyance faded fast when he got a good look at Garrett's expression.

"Dude, we're having some private time here."

"Dude," Garrett corrected through gritted teeth. "You're done. Take off."

Alex whipped her windblown hair out of her face and glared at him. "Go away, Garrett."

Astonished, the handsome guy stared at her. "You know this guy?"

"Yes, but pay no attention to him," Alex said.

Garrett's hand on Blondie's shoulder tightened as he silently convinced the other man it would be a much better idea to disappear. Fast.

Message received.

"Yeah, right. Okay. Outta here." He hunched away from Garrett's grip, gave Alex a wistful look and shrugged. "Sorry, babe. I don't do violence. I think *he* does."

"Damn straight," Garrett assured him.

"Oh, for—" Alex set her hands at her hips and glared at Garrett as Blondie hurried back to the restaurant, in search of easier prey. "What do you think you're doing?"

"Hah!" Garrett backed her up against the railing, looming over her as he planted his hands at either side of her. His grip on the cold, damp, iron railing tightened as he looked down into her eyes. "What am I doing? I'm keeping you from getting mauled in public."

"We were hardly in public and what if I *liked* being mauled?" she snapped, her eyes flashing with the kind of heat that any sane man would accept as a warning.

Garrett, though, had passed "sane" a couple of exits back. He was too close to her, bodies aligned, that damn dress of hers displaying way too much beautiful, smooth skin. Heat seared his insides and his dick went to stone. Just the scent of her was enough to drive him insane. He fought for clarity. Fought for control.

"Damn it, Alex. I get that you're pissed at me. And fine. I can deal with it."

"Oh, how very gracious of you."

"But," he continued, leaning close enough that her breasts were pillowed against his chest. That she could feel his erection pressing into her abdomen. Her eyes widened and her lips parted on a sigh. "I'm not going to stand around and watch you make a mistake."

"Another one, you mean?"

In the background, the music was soft, tempting; the singer's voice a lure, drawing them into a world where it was just the two of them, locked together. He felt every inch of her luscious body aligned along his. And in a heartbeat, control and focus went out the window, and Garrett found he couldn't even give a good damn.

"You didn't want that guy's hands on you, Alex."

She let her head fall back. Her eyes met his and a long sigh slid from her throat. "Is that right? And how do you know that?"

"Because you want *my* hands on you," he muttered, his gaze raking over her features before settling on her eyes. "You want *me* touching you and no one else."

She opened her mouth to say something, but Garrett didn't let her speak. Instead, he cupped her face in his hands, leaned down and took her mouth with his.

Pissed or not, Alex wanted him, too. He felt it in her instant surrender. She wrapped her arms around his neck, held his head to her and gave him everything she had. Their tongues entwined, caressing, stroking. The cool air swept past them, and danced across their heated skin.

She shivered, and he wrapped his arms around her,

holding her closer, tighter, until he felt her frenzied heartbeat racing in time with his own. Every inch of his skin hummed with anticipation.

He knew they had been headed for this moment since the day they had met. It didn't matter that he had fought it. This was inevitable. Pulling his head back, he looked down into her glassy eyes and whispered, "Your hotel's only a few minutes from here."

Dragging in a breath, she shivered again and leaned into him. "Then why are we still standing here?"

A fierce grin split his face briefly. Then he took her hand and headed around the edge of the balcony toward the front of the place. Now he was glad he hadn't bothered with valet parking. He didn't have the patience to hang around while some kid ran to bring him his car.

No more waiting.

That first taste of her pushed him over the edge. Touching her wouldn't be enough this time.

This time, he had to have it all.

Nine

It was minutes that felt like hours.

Desire pumping in the air around them, making each heartbeat sound like a gong in their heads, the drive to Alex's hotel was bristling with sexual heat. Somehow, Garrett got the car parked, and Alex through the lobby into the private elevator. Somehow, they managed to walk through the door of the penthouse and slam it closed behind them.

And then all bets were off.

Hunger was king here and neither of them had the strength or the will to fight it any longer.

Garrett tore off his jacket and tossed it aside. Alex's hands fumbled at the buttons on his shirt while he ripped his tie off and discarded it, as well. The moment his shirt was undone, her hands moved over his chest and every one of her fingers felt as if it were imprinting itself on his skin. Heat sizzled back and forth between them, leaving each of them struggling for air. Sighs and groans were the only sounds as they kissed again, hungrily, frantically.

He stabbed his fingers through her wild mane of hair and let the silkiness slide across his skin like cool water. She opened her mouth under his, offering him everything and he took it. Garrett was through pretending that their relationship was strictly business.

At least for this one night, he wanted everything that he had been dreaming of, thinking of, for the past several days. He couldn't touch her enough. Couldn't kiss her enough. He wanted more. Wanted all. Had to have her.

"Now, Alex," he muttered, tearing his mouth from hers to drag his lips and tongue and teeth along the elegant sweep of her neck.

She sighed and tipped her head to one side, as she held his head to her throat. "Yes, Garrett. Yes, please, *now*."

He unzipped the back of her dress and pushed the slender straps down her arms, letting it fall to the floor at her feet. She stepped out of the puddle of fabric and kicked it to one side.

"You're amazing," he whispered, gaze moving over her as she stood there, naked but for those high heels she loved and a tiny scrap of black lace panties. She looked like every man's fantasy and she was his. All his.

Garrett caught her, pulled her in close, then bent his head to take first one then the other erect, pink nipple into his mouth. Her fingers threaded through his hair and pressed his head to her breasts as if afraid he would stop.

He had no intention of stopping.

The taste of her filled him. Her scent surrounded him. A haze settled over his mind, shutting out everything but the present. All there was in the world was this woman.

His hands moved over her skin, up and down her back, around and across her abdomen to the tiny scrap of black lace she wore. His fingers gave a sharp tug and she was naked, open for his touch.

Still suckling at her, he dropped one hand to the juncture of her thighs and sighed against her when she parted her legs for him. He stroked that single bud of pleasure until she was whimpering and rocking against his hand. Her hips twisted and moved in time with his touch, and he smiled against her breast as he felt her climax build.

Lifting his head, he stared at her as his fingers worked her body into a frenzy. She licked her lips, tossed her hair back and took breath after greedy breath.

Her gaze locked with his and her voice was soft as she said, "I want you inside me this time, Garrett. I need to feel you inside me."

He wouldn't have thought he could get any harder. But he did. Reluctantly, he let her go just long enough to strip out of his clothes. He paused only long enough to take a condom from his wallet and sheathe himself. When she made to kick off her high heels, though, he shook his head. "Leave 'em on."

She gave him a slow, wide smile, then dropped her gaze to take in all of him. Her eyes widened and when she looked up at him again, she was even more eager for him. "Now, Garrett. Be with me. Be *in* me."

They were still in the damn living room of the suite and Garrett knew that they'd never make it to the bedroom. Neither of them was willing to wait that long.

He swept her close to him and when his erection pushed at her, she moaned and moved into him, feeding the fires that were already swallowing him. "That's it. Right here, right now. We'll do it slow next time."

"Next time," she agreed.

He carried her a few short steps to the couch, set her on the high back and stepped in between her thighs. She opened herself wider for him and when he entered her, Alex groaned aloud.

Garrett gritted his teeth to keep from shouting as his body invaded hers in one hard thrust. Her damp heat enveloped him, a tight glove, squeezing. When he was seated to the hilt, Alex held him even closer. She moved on the precarious edge of the couch as much as she could. Now she did kick off those heels so she could lock her legs around his hips and hold on as he set a fast, dizzying pace that pushed them both as high as they could go.

They raced to the edge together. Gazes locked, bodies joined, two halves of the same whole. Again and again, his hips pistoned against her and she took everything he had, urging him on.

As the first crash of her orgasm slammed into her, she called out his name and Garrett felt her body spasm around his. He watched her shatter, felt the strength of her climax shaking her. And Garrett realized he'd never known this before. Never been this connected to any woman before. He watched her pleasure and felt it as his own.

He heard her sighs and wanted to capture them forever. Heard his name on her lips and felt both humbled and victorious. Possession raged through him and his only thought as his own release finally claimed him was: *mine.*

Seconds ticked past, became minutes, and those could have been hours for all Alex knew. Or cared.

With Garrett's body still locked with hers, she had everything she had been craving for days. The incredible feel of him deep inside her. The dazzling orgasm that was so much better than anything she had ever felt before. The sweet sensation of his arms wrapped around her. It was all…perfect.

As if she really had found the magic she had been looking for when she first began this holiday.

But even as that thought flitted through her mind, she

knew it wasn't true. Despite what she was feeling, she knew now that Garrett didn't share it.

Want wasn't romance.

Desire wasn't love.

Love? Now where had that thought come from? She stiffened in his arms as the word circled round and round in her mind. She didn't want to believe it, but how could she not? What she felt for Garrett was so far beyond what she had ever known with anyone else.

What else could it be, but love?

Which put her in a very uncomfortable position.

She was in love with a man who was only with her because he had been hired by her father.

"Alex..." Garrett's voice thundered down around her, sounding like a summer storm, and she knew that their moment was over.

She looked up at him, watching his face as he spoke again.

"I'm sorry."

She blinked. "You're *sorry?*"

He pulled away from her and she instantly missed the feeling of his body pressed into hers. And she wanted to kick herself for it. How could she possibly love such a Neanderthal?

"It shouldn't have happened," he muttered, raking one hand through his hair and stepping back so she could slide off the back of the couch. "I let myself be distracted and allowed you to do the same."

"Allowed?" she echoed. "You *allowed* me?"

He didn't pick up on the temper in her voice, or if he did, he wasn't paying attention. His mistake.

"I take full responsibility for this, and I want you to know, it won't happen again."

"You...you..." She opened and closed her mouth several times, but nothing came out. Well, who knew that "stunned speechless" could actually happen? Her bare toes curled into the rug beneath her feet as if she needed all the help she could get just to keep her balance.

"I know what you're going to say," he told her, with a small, brief smile. "And you don't have to. I know you regret this as much as I do."

Oh, she wanted to do something to wipe that "understanding" expression off his face. But once again, her breeding rang true and she settled for quietly seething instead. When she could speak again, she did so quietly. "So you're writing my dialogue for me as well, are you?"

"What?"

Fury flashed inside her like an electrical storm. She actually *felt* bolts of white-hot anger stabbing through her system, and it was all she could do to keep from screaming. Looking up at him, Alex shook her head and said, "You pompous, arrogant, dim-witted, ego-maniacal... *twit!*"

He scowled at her. "What the hell?"

"Oh," she said, eyes widely innocent. "Weren't expecting that, were you?"

"What are you so pissed about *now?*"

"The very fact that you could even ask me that proves your twit-dom!"

"That's not even a word."

"It is now," she told him, stalking a few paces away because she was simply so furious she couldn't stand still. She should have been embarrassed, or, at the very least, uncomfortable, walking about her suite stark naked. But truthfully, she was too angry to care.

"I'm trying to do the right thing," he said, each word grinding out of his throat.

"For the both of us, it seems," she snapped. Her gaze

fixed on him, she said, "Did it even occur to you that what I might regret most is your ridiculous attitude?"

"Ridiculous? I'm taking responsibility for this mess. How is that ridiculous?"

"How is this a *mess?*" she countered.

"You know damn well how," he muttered. "Because I'm here to protect you."

"But not from pompous asses, apparently," she said.

"Okay, that's enough."

"Have you decided that, as well?" she asked, a sugary sweet tone to her voice.

"What the hell, Alex? We both know this shouldn't have happened."

"So sayeth the almighty arbiter of everything sexual."

"You're starting to piss me off."

"Well, join the bloody club!" Walking back to him, she stopped within a foot of his gorgeous body, tipped her head back and glared into those eyes that only moments ago had been glazed with passion. Now there were ice chips in those depths and damned if she didn't find them just as attractive. "I'm not a naive young virgin out for her first romp in the hay, you know. You're not the first man in my bed. You're simply the first to regret it the moment it was over. Well, thank you very much for that, Garrett King.

"Now, why don't you take your sense of responsibility and leave?"

"I'm not going anywhere until we settle this."

"Then I hope you packed a lunch," she quipped, "because I don't see that happening anytime soon."

"Maybe if you'd be reasonable…"

She sucked in a gulp of air and gave him a shove. He didn't budge an inch. Like shoving a bloody wall. "Reasonable? You think I'm *not* being reasonable? It's only my exceptional breeding and the training of my mother, not to mention countless governesses, that's keeping me from punching you in the nose!"

He laughed at the very idea, which infuriated her enough to curl her hand into a fist and take a wild swing at him, just as her brothers had taught her to. Garrett, though, was too fast for her and caught her hand in his before she could make contact.

"Nice 'breeding,'" he said with a half smile.

"You're insufferable."

"You've said that before."

"Then clearly I'm an astute human being."

He sighed. "Alex, look me in the eye and tell me you think this was a good thing. I'm not looking for a relationship. This is going nowhere."

His words slapped her, but she wouldn't let him see it. She wouldn't be the needy one while he tried to make light of something that had shaken her to her very foundations. So she took a page from his book…she lied. "What makes you think I'm looking for a future with you? Are you really that egotistical? Do you think one night in bed with you is enough to make a woman immediately start craving white picket fences? Start scribbling her name next to yours surrounded by lacy hearts?

"I'm a *princess,* Garrett. I may have run off for a holiday but I know what my duties are. I know what my life will be. God knows, it was planned for me practically from the moment I drew my first breath! And nowhere in that plan does it say *fall in love with a Neanderthal, move to California and remain barefoot and pregnant.*"

Her breath was coming fast, in and out of her lungs. Her heartbeat was racing and her blood was pumping. Being this close to him was feeding more than her anger. In spite of everything, she wanted him.

He was stupid and clueless and impossibly arrogant—and, he was the most intriguing man she had ever known. Even the fact that he had lied to her from the beginning wasn't enough to cool off the fires licking at her insides. And Alex had the distinct feeling that thirty years from now, when he was nothing more than a hazy memory, she would *still* want him.

"Neanderthal?"

Her fury abated for the moment, she only asked, "How would you describe yourself at this moment?"

"Confused, angry—" he paused, tucked his fingers beneath her chin and lifted her face, her eyes, up to his "—and more turned on than I was before."

He felt it, too. That soul-deep stirring. He didn't want it, either, but it seemed as though neither of them had a choice when it came to what lay sizzling between them. Arguments didn't matter. Differences didn't matter.

All that mattered was the next touch. The next kiss.

"Oh," she admitted on a sigh, "me, too."

He kissed her and the rest of the world fell away. Alex let go of her anger and gave herself up to the wonder of what he could make her feel.

His arms came around her as his mouth took hers. He carried her into the bedroom and laid her down atop the silk duvet. The slide of the cool fabric against her skin was just another sensation to pile onto the rest.

Sliding his hands up and down her body, Alex arched into him, allowing her mind to drift free so that she could concentrate solely on the moment. Every stroke was a benediction. Every caress a promise of more to come.

Her body felt alive in a way it never had before. His touch was magic…kindling sparks of flame at every spot he touched. He leaned over her, kissing her, then sliding along her body, nibbling his way down. Then he stopped, pulled back and slid off the bed.

"Where are you going?"

"Right back," he swore, his eyes fixed on hers.

True to his word, he was gone only moments and she saw that he had another condom with him, sheathing himself as he came closer.

A smile tugged at the corner of her mouth. "You always carry those in your wallet?"

"I have since I met you," he admitted, kneeling back on the bed, dropping his head for a quick kiss. "Just in case."

"Always prepared?" she asked.

"Babe, those are the Boy Scouts. And trust me when I say I'm no Boy Scout."

"No," she whispered as he moved down the length of her body again, letting his mouth and tongue blaze the trail, "you're really not."

Alex sighed deeply and stared up at the ceiling. Moonlight poured through the windows, along with a chill ocean breeze that ruffled the white sheers and sent them into a sensual dance that mimicked her own movements beneath Garrett's talented hands.

"You're torturing me," she whispered and arched into him as his lips crossed over her abdomen.

"That's the plan," Garrett assured her.

"You're an evil man," she said on a sigh. "Don't stop."

"Not a chance," he promised.

Then he moved, shifting down to kneel between her thighs and Alex looked at him. Slowly he scooped his hands beneath her bottom and lifted her from the bed. Everything in her tensed in expectation. Her gaze locked with his as he lowered his mouth to her center and—

She groaned at the first sweep of his tongue across a bud of flesh so sensitive it felt as if it had a life of its own.

Electric-like jolts of sensation shot through her, coiling
the tension within her even tighter. Alex moved into him,
loving the feel of his mouth on her.

Reaching down, she pushed her fingers through his
hair as he pushed her higher and faster than she had gone
before. This intimacy was so overwhelming; her system
was flooded with emotions tangling together. She felt so
much, wanted so much, *needed* so much.

It was close. She felt it. The orgasm hovering just out
of reach was almost on her and she wanted him inside her
when it hit. "Garrett, please."

Instantly, he pulled away from her, sat back on his
thighs and lifted her onto his lap. Alex went up onto her
knees and slowly, deliberately, lowered herself onto him.
It was delicious. The tantalizingly slow slide of his hard
thickness pushing into her depths. She gloried in every
inch of him. She let her head fall back as she wrapped her
arms around his neck and swiveled her hips against him,
taking him even higher and deeper than she had before.

Until she was sure he was touching the tip of her heart.

"You feel so good," he whispered, kissing the base
of her throat, locking his lips against her pulse point.
His breath hot against her skin, he whispered words she
couldn't hear—could only *feel*.

And then she moved on him and his hands settled at her
hips, guiding her motions, helping her set a rhythm they
both kept time with. Again and again, she rocked her body
onto his, and, over and over, they tore apart and came together. They moved as one. Breathed as one.

And at last, they shattered as one.

Ten

In the dark, when it was quiet, reality crashed down on top of them again, and Alex was the first to feel its sharp tugs at the edges of her heart.

Grabbing up her short, blue silk robe, she slipped it on, then crossed her bedroom, opened the French doors leading to the balcony that wrapped around the entire penthouse suite and stepped outside. The stone floor was cool and damp beneath her feet and the wind off the ocean lifted her hair and teased her heated skin.

Staring out at the moonlit sea, Alex tried to get a handle on the rampaging emotions crashing through her. Her mind was alive with careening thoughts that rushed up to be noticed then were swallowed and replaced by the next one. In fact, the only thing she was truly sure of was that she did love Garrett King. Infuriating as he was, she loved him.

They'd known each other such a short time, it was hard

to believe. But the simple fact was, as her mother had always told her, love didn't come with a timetable. It was either there or it wasn't and no amount of waiting would change that.

Her heart ached and her mind whirled. There was misery along this road and she knew it. Garrett had made no secret of the fact that he wasn't interested in a relationship. And even if he were, their lives were so different. They didn't even live on the same *continent!* What possible chance was there for anything more than what they had already shared?

Taking hold of the iron railing in front of her, she squeezed tightly in response to the tension within.

A moment later, Garrett joined her, and her heart sped into a gallop. She glanced at him. He was wearing the slacks he'd abandoned what felt like hours ago, but he was barefoot and shirtless and his broad, sculpted chest seemed to be begging for her touch. She gripped the handrails to keep from giving in to that urge.

"Alex, we really need to talk."

"That never bodes well," she replied, deliberately turning her gaze on the ever-shifting surface of the water below.

He stood beside her. Close, but not touching and still, she felt the heat from his body sliding into hers.

"It's too late to do a damn thing about it, but none of that should have happened, Alex."

She stiffened. He still regretted being with her. How would he react, she wondered, if he knew she loved him? She glanced over the railing to the sand ten stories below. He'd probably jump.

"No doubt you're right."

"Huh." She felt more than saw him turn his gaze on her. "You surprise me. I expected a different reaction."

Alex steeled herself then turned to look up into his eyes. "What were you thinking? Keening? Gnashing of teeth?" She gave him a smile that felt stiff and wooden. "Sorry to disappoint."

"Not disappointed. Just surprised."

"Well, you shouldn't be," she said, silently congratulating herself on how calm and cool she sounded. Honestly, if she weren't a princess, she should think of going on the stage. "You'd already made yourself quite clear on the subject, and, as I've mentioned, I'm not an idiot, Garrett. I know that we don't suit. I know we mean nothing to each other and that this isn't going anywhere...."

Those words ripped a new hole in the fabric of her heart, but better *she* say them than him.

"I didn't say you mean nothing to me, Alex," he said, laying his hands on her shoulders and turning her so that she faced him.

God, she didn't want to look into his eyes. Didn't want to feel the heat of him spearing through her body. Didn't want to think about the pain she would feel when she was gone and back in the palace.

The only way to get through any of it was to pretend none of it mattered.

So she gave him that forced smile again and hoped he wouldn't notice. "Ah, yes, I forgot," she quipped. "I do mean something to you after all. Quite a hefty paycheck, I'm guessing."

"I didn't say that, either," he ground out.

"You haven't said much, Garrett," she told him. "What else am I to think?"

"That you're an amazing, smart, funny, incredibly sexy *princess*."

"It always comes back to that, doesn't it?" she mused, stepping out of his grip and turning to face the sea again.

"If I'd known how you would focus on that, I would have worn my crown while we were in bed together."

"I don't give a damn for your crown, Alex," he snapped, voice near growling now. "In fact this would all be a hell of a lot easier if you *weren't* a princess. You think your father would be thrilled to know that I'm here with you?"

"What's my father got to do with any of this?"

Clearly exasperated, he snapped, "I've done security work for royalty all over the globe. You know what's the *one* thing they all have in common? They don't get involved with non-royals. Hell, I've got more money than a lot of them, but I'm still a 'commoner.' You think your father feels any different?"

"Probably not."

"Exactly." Garrett shook his head. "It all comes down to that, Princess."

"Story of my life," she murmured, sliding a glance at him.

"What's that supposed to mean?"

"Please," she scoffed. "Do you think you're the only man who has run screaming into the night trying to escape the glare of the palace? You're not." Shaking her head she added, "And for all of those that run away, dozens more run *toward* the crown. None of them see me, Alex. They see the princess. Some hate the very idea of royalty and others covet it. People on the outside look at the royal family and think, *Isn't it wonderful? All the pomp and pageantry. How nice to shop wherever you like and not worry about the price.*

"Well," she continued, "there's *always* a price, Garrett. It's just one that most people never see. It's a lack of privacy. A lack of freedom and imagination. It's being locked into centuries of tradition whether you like it or not, and it's duty."

Her gaze narrowed, her breath coming fast and furious, she hurried on before he could say a word. She looked up into his eyes and watched them flash with emotion, but she didn't let that stop her.

"You think I don't understand your 'duty' to protect me? Trust me when I say that's the one thing I am all too aware of. Duty is the first thing I was taught. Duty to my country, to the citizens of Cadria and to my king. My family has ruled for centuries. Yes, Cadria is a small country, but she's proud and it's *our* duty to protect her. Keep her safe. So, yes. I understand your self-imposed duties, but it doesn't mean I like them any more than I like the golden chains linking me to my own set of duties."

He studied her for a long minute before speaking. When he did, he said only, "Quite a rant."

She huffed out a short laugh. "Apparently, I have what you Americans refer to as 'issues.'"

"I never use that word," he assured her, and reached out for her again.

Smiling, she let herself be held. Probably another monumental mistake, but she needed the comfort of his arms. The strength of him, wrapped around her. If she had one more thing to regret in the morning, then so be it.

"Why'd your father have to be a *king?*"

She laughed a little and linked her arms at the small of his back. "Your father was a King, too."

He gave her a squeeze. "Funny."

Tipping her head back, she looked up at him and whispered, "You may be willing to pretend that everything that happened tonight was a mistake, but I for one, enjoyed myself immensely."

"So did I, Alex. That's the problem."

"Doesn't have to be."

He shook his head. "I'm here to do a job and that doesn't include bedding *you*."

That barb hit home with a staggering force she didn't even want to admit to herself. So much for tender makeup scenes in the moonlight. "Yes," she said softly. "I wonder if you'll get a raise in pay for this? Maybe if I tell my father how very good you were?"

"Cut it out, Alex."

She felt like a fool. She'd spilled her heart out to him, laid it at his feet and he chose that moment to remind her that he was being paid by her father. How could she possibly *love* a man who only saw her as a job? How could she have forgotten, even for a minute, that he had lied to her from their first day together? That her father was paying him to watch over her?

Well, fine. If he wanted to turn his back on what they had together, then she wouldn't stop him. She might be fool enough to love him, but she wasn't so big a fool that she didn't know when to pull back from the edge of a very steep cliff. Releasing him, she steeled herself for the soul-deep cold that slipped inside her the instant she left the circle of his arms.

"You're the one who brought this up again," she reminded him.

"I just want you to understand is all. I didn't want to say yes to your dad, but he's a hard man to refuse."

"That much I know from personal experience."

He took a breath. "When I realized who you were, I was worried. I called your father and told him I was uncomfortable with you out on your own with no protection. And so was he. I talked to your mother, too."

She closed her eyes briefly and he felt the tension in her body tighten. "So they double-teamed you."

"Yeah," he said with a sharp nod. "Guess you could say that."

"They're very good at it," she mused, a half smile blooming and disappearing from her mouth in a fraction of a second. "It's how they deal with my brothers and me, as well."

"Then you can see why—"

"I can see why you said yes to my father," she cut him off neatly and speared him with a glance that had gone icy. "What I don't see is why you *lied* to me."

"I lied because I had to. Your father told me you're adept at escaping your guards."

"And because you lied, I never even tried to escape you," she whispered.

"I couldn't risk you escaping me, Alex. I had to keep you safe. As for fighting what was happening between us..." He paused and shook his head again as if he couldn't believe they were in this situation. "In my job, when I get distracted, people tend to *die.* I won't let that happen to you, Alex."

"Garrett, if you don't *live,* you might as well be dead already. Don't you see that?"

"What I see is that I let you get to me," he said, gaze moving over her face. "Didn't mean to. Didn't want you to. But you did anyway."

A part of her thrilled to hear it. But the more rational voice in her mind warned against it. The look in his eyes was far from warm and fuzzy. The set of his jaw and the tension in every line of his body screamed that he was a man who'd made his decision. Alex had come in second to his sense of honor. What he said next only defined it.

"As much as I want you, I can't let this happen again, Alex. Not while I'm responsible for your safety."

There it was. Duty first. She should respect that sentiment, seeing as she had been raised to believe the same. But somehow, that didn't make her feel any better.

A chill swept over her that had nothing at all to do with the cold wind still flying toward them. Garrett couldn't have made himself clearer.

"No worries, Garrett," she told him, keeping her voice light in spite of the knot of pain clogging her throat. "You're absolutely safe from me now as I'm just not interested anymore."

"Liar."

She laughed shortly. "Amazing that you even feel comfortable using that word against someone else."

"Amazing that you can be so pissed at me for doing something you're pretty good at yourself."

She ignored that and turned for the bedroom, suddenly more than ready for this conversation to be over. "Before you go, want to check the bathroom for hidden assassins?"

"Funny."

Stepping into the bedroom, she walked to the dressing table, picked up her hairbrush and started drawing the bristles through her tangled hair. Staring into the mirror, she caught his reflected gaze. "You're making far too much of this situation. You're assuming I want this 'relationship' to continue. But I don't."

"Lying again."

She tossed the brush down. "Stop telling me when I'm lying. It's rude."

"Then stop lying."

"Same to you."

"I'm not lying now," he said. "I still want you."

"Me, too."

"Damn it, Alex."

"Shut up and kiss me, Garrett."

He did and Alex's brain went on hiatus again. Soon,

she would be able to sit back and regret this at her leisure. But at the moment, all she could think was how right it felt. How good it was to be in his arms again. To have his mouth fused to hers.

He lifted her and carried her to the bed and when he set her down onto the mattress, she looked up into icy-blue eyes that sparked and shone with the kind of need that shook her to the bone.

For now, that was enough.

Three days later, Garrett was on the edge with no way out.

Now that she knew who he was, Alex seemed to delight in making him nuts. She insisted on walking down crowded sidewalks, going shopping through packed malls and even driving to San Diego to visit SeaWorld. It was as if she had determined to make him earn every dime of his paycheck from her father.

It was a security expert's nightmare.

Garrett knew damn well it was only a matter of time before her identity was revealed. Someone, somewhere, was going to recognize her and then he'd be hip-deep in paparazzi, reporters and general nutcases, all trying to get close to the visiting princess.

But short of locking her into her penthouse, he didn't have a clue how to keep her from being noticed. A woman like Alex got people's attention. She was tall, gorgeous and had a perpetual smile on her face that seemed to welcome conversations with strangers. He hovered as closely as he could and still it wasn't enough.

His mind filled with ugly possibilities. He'd seen enough damage done over the years to be prepared for the absolute worst—his brain dredging up any number of horrific scenarios. And it killed him to think of anything happening to Alex.

Which was only natural, he assured himself. After all, she was in his care. Of course he'd be worried about her—that was his *job*. And that was all it was.

Garrett's trained gaze swept the room as he deliberately tried to become invisible, as any good bodyguard would. But, being the only man in a homeless shelter that catered to women and kids made Garrett's job harder. He stood out like Death at the Party. He caught the glances tossed his way and was sorry to know he was making some of the women here really uncomfortable. But damned if he was going to let Alex out of his sight.

The woman continued to press her luck and push him closer and closer to the ragged edge of control. Today, she had insisted on visiting a women's shelter to compare their setup with the program she knew at home.

Jane, the woman in charge, hadn't had a problem with his presence—but she had asked him to stay out of the way and that he was willing to do. Better all the way around for a protection detail to blend into the background as much as possible. It gave him eyes and ears to the place without attracting attention himself.

Watching Alex move around the room with the director, Garrett felt his admiration for her grow. She wasn't here as a princess. She had introduced herself as a fellow volunteer, visiting from Europe. And in a few short minutes, she and Jane had been chatting like old friends.

While Alex looked at the facility and met a few of the residents, Garrett watched *her*. She fit in any damn where, he thought and wondered at how easily Alex dismissed *what* she was in favor of *who* she was. She was so much more than some dilettante royal. She was eager and involved and she *cared* for people and what she might do to help. It had nothing to do with her crown. This was her soul he was watching, and damned if he could look away.

"You a cop?"

Garrett jolted out of his daydreams, gave himself a mental kick for being caught unaware and then looked down at the little boy staring up at him with wide brown eyes. "No, I'm not a cop."

"Look like one," the boy said, giving Garrett a gap-toothed smile. "You're all straight and stiff like one."

Great. He was doing such a good job being invisible that a five-year-old had made him. Alex really was throwing him off his game.

One corner of his mouth lifted in a smile. "You stand up straight, you get taller."

Those brown eyes went as big as saucers. "Tall as you?"

"Taller," Garrett assured him and instantly, the kid squared his shoulders, straightened his spine and lifted his chin. All forty pounds of him.

"Is she your girlfriend?"

That question came unexpectedly, though why it had, he didn't know. He'd spent enough time around his cousin's kids to know that they said pretty much whatever popped into their heads. "No," he said, shifting his gaze back to Alex. "She's a friend."

"She's nice," the boy said. "Pretty, too, and she smells good."

"Yeah," Garrett said, still watching Alex. "You're right."

"You should make her your girlfriend."

Intrigued, he shot the kid a look and asked, "Yeah? Why's that?"

"Because she smiles when she looks at you and that's nice. Besides, she's *pretty*."

"Timmy!" A woman shouted from across the room and the little boy trotted off, leaving Garrett staring after him.

Out of the mouths of babes, he mused. He looked up, caught Alex's eye and she flashed him one of those smiles that seemed designed to knock him off balance. In a flash, he remembered her under him, over him. The feel of her skin, the taste of her mouth, the scent of her, surrounding him.

As if she knew exactly what he was thinking, her smile slipped into something more private. More…intimate. And Garrett was once again hit with the knowledge that he'd fallen into a hole that just kept getting deeper.

Alex very much enjoyed watching Garrett go quietly insane at the beach. It was a lovely day to sit on the sand and enjoy the last of summer. There were only a handful of people there, including a few children busily building sand walls in an attempt to hold back the inexorable rush of the tide. Sandpipers and seagulls strutted along the shoreline and surfers sat atop their boards waiting for the perfect ride.

Everyone was having a good time, she thought. Everyone, that is, but Garrett King.

Honestly, it was simply too easy to push the man's buttons. And Alex had discovered just how much fun it could be. The man was determined to keep her at a distance. He hadn't touched her since that one night they'd spent together. Her heart hurt and her body ached for his and so, she had decided to make him as uncomfortable as possible with his decision to leave her alone.

If she was going to be miserable, then she would do everything she could to make sure he was, too. She challenged him, worried him and in general made his time with her as difficult as possible. She flirted with him outrageously and watched him fight his own desires to keep his professionalism at the fore.

With his serious "bodyguard" expression, he kept most people at bay. But those who weren't the least bit intimidated slipped past him, much to Alex's delight. Because then she flirted with other men, just to watch Garrett's instant, infuriated response.

Take for example the surfer who was right now giving her a wink and a smile before heading for the water. If she weren't in love with a perfectly infuriating man, she would very well be tempted to take the other man up on his not-so-subtle offer.

"He's short," Garrett muttered from behind her.

She smiled to herself, nodded at the surfer and said, "He's at least six feet tall."

"Shorter than me, then," Garrett said tightly.

"Most people are," she returned. "Hardly a crime."

"He's at least thirty and he's at the beach in the middle of the week."

"So are you," she pointed out, glancing over her shoulder at the man in black who was glowering at the rest of humanity. Honestly, he looked like the Grim Reaper. No wonder most people tended to give her a wide berth.

"Yes, but I'm *working*," he told her.

"And you never let me forget that, do you?" Alex gritted her teeth and turned her head back to watch the handsome surfer carry his board out to the water. His black wet suit clung to a fairly amazing body and his long, light brown hair was sun-streaked, telling her he spent most of his days in the sun. Perhaps Garrett was right and he was a layabout. She frowned at the thought.

"Alex, don't start that again."

"I didn't start it, Garrett," she told him, now ignoring the surfer to concentrate on the conversation she was having with the man who refused to get close to her. "I never do. You're the one who consistently reminds me that I'm your *responsibility*. And I simply can't tell you how flattering that is."

He sighed. She heard it even from three feet away.

"But, even though it's your *job* to watch over me," she added, not for the first time, "it doesn't give you the right to chase away any man who dares to look at me."

"It is if I think they're dangerous."

She laughed outright at that comment and turned to stare at him. "Like the college student yesterday at the art gallery? That sweet young man who was so nervous he dropped his bottle of water?"

Garrett frowned. "He kept touching you."

"It was *crowded* in that shop."

"That's what he wanted you to think. He wasn't nervous, Alex. He was on the prowl. He kept bumping into you. *Touching* you." Scowling, he picked up a handful of sand and let it drift through his fingers. "It wasn't that crowded."

"Well, certainly not after you threw the poor soul up against a wall and frisked him!"

He smiled at the memory. "Did discourage him quick enough, didn't it?"

"And half the gallery," she pointed out. "People scattered, thinking you were a crazy person."

"Yeah..." He was still smiling.

"You're impossible. You know that, don't you?"

"If I hadn't known it before I met you, I do now. You tell me often enough."

"And yet you don't listen." Pushing up from the sand, Alex dusted off the seat of her white shorts and snatched up the sandals she had kicked off when they first arrived. Walking to him, she looked down into Garrett's eyes and said, "You might want to ask yourself why you take it so personally when another man looks at me. Or talks to me."

"You know why," he muttered, keeping his gaze fixed on hers.

"Yes, the job." She went down to one knee in front of him. "But I think it's more than that, Garrett. I think it's much more, but you're too much of a coward to admit it."

His features went like granite, and Alex knew she'd struck a nerve. Well, good. Happy to know it.

So quickly she hardly saw him move, he reached out, grabbed her and pulled her close. Then he gave her a brief, hard kiss before letting her go again. Shaking his head, he stood up, then took her hand and drew her to her feet as well.

"You keep pushing me, Alex, and you never know what might happen."

"And that, Garrett," she said, licking her lips and giving him a small victory smile, "is the fun part."

Eleven

"I quit."

"I beg your pardon?"

Garrett winced at the snooty tone the King of Cadria could produce. He had known going in that this phone call wouldn't go well, but there was nothing to be done about it. Garrett was through working for the king, and Alex's father was just going to have to deal with it.

"You heard me correctly, your majesty," he said, leaning back in his desk chair. The study in his home was dark, filled with shadows in every corner. A single lamp on his desk wasn't enough to chase them away—seemed like a pretty good metaphor for his life at the moment, he thought, surprised at the poetic train his mind was taking. But there were shadows in Garrett's past, too. Always there. Always ready to pounce. And the light that was Alex—though damn brighter than anything he'd ever known—still couldn't get rid of all those dark places.

So there was really only one thing to do. "I quit as your daughter's bodyguard."

The king blustered and shouted and Garrett let him go. He figured he owed it to the man to let him get it all out of his system. And while a royal father thousands of miles away ranted and raged, Garrett's mind turned to that afternoon on the beach. The look in Alex's eyes. The taste of her.

These past few days had been torturous. He couldn't be with her without wanting her and he couldn't have her as long as he was responsible for her safety. But the whole truth was, he couldn't have her, *period.*

Even if he gave in to what he wanted, what would it gain either of them? Soon she'd be going home to a damn palace. He would be here, in California running his business. He wasn't looking to be in love or to be married. But even if he were, she was a princess and there was just no way Garrett could compete with that. Oh, he was rich enough to give her the kind of house and servants she was used to. But he didn't have the pedigree her family would expect of a man wanting to be with Alex.

He was a King, and he was damn proud of it. The problem was, she was the daughter of a *king.*

No. There was nothing ahead for them but more misery and, thanks very much, but he'd rather skip that part of the festivities.

Sitting forward, he braced his elbow on the desktop and only half listened to the king on the other end of the line. Whatever the man said wouldn't change Garrett's mind. He already knew he was doing the only thing possible. For both of them.

"Mr. King," Alex's father was sputtering, "you cannot simply walk away from my daughter's safety without so much as a warning. I will need time to—"

Enough was enough.

"Sir, I won't take money from you to watch over Alex," Garrett finally interrupted the king and the other man's abrupt silence told him the king wasn't used to that kind of treatment. Just one more nugget of proof that Garrett King and royalty were never going to be a good mix. "But, that said," he continued into the quiet, "I won't leave her out there alone, either. On my own, I'll watch out for her until she's on a plane headed home."

"May I ask *why* you've decided to leave my employ?"

Touchy question, Garrett told himself. He could hardly confess to the king that he didn't want to be taking money from the father of the woman he wanted in his bed. That might be enough for a beheading in Cadria, for all Garrett knew.

"Let's just say, Alex and I have become friends. And I feel badly taking money from her father."

There was a long silence, and then the king gave a tired sigh. Garrett sympathized. Couldn't be easy being thousands of miles away from someone you worried about. "Fine then. I appreciate your help in this, Mr. King, and it won't be forgotten."

Long after the king hung up, Garrett sat in his darkened study and stared at nothing. No, he thought. None of this would be forgotten.

Ever.

The late-night knock on Alex's door startled her.

She tossed the book she had been reading to the sofa cushion beside her. Jumping up from the couch, she tugged at the belt of her blue silk robe and crossed the room with hesitant steps. She wasn't expecting anyone and the desk always called before they disturbed her. And just who would have been able to get onto the penthouse elevator besides… She looked through the peephole and saw Garrett staring back at her.

Her heart did a slow roll in her chest as her nerves drained away and an entirely different emotion charged to the surface. She leaned her forehead on the cool, painted surface of the door and took a breath. Would the man always have this effect on her? Would one look at him always be enough to turn her knees to water?

Shaking her head, she steadied herself, then fumbled with the locks and opened the door to him. "Garrett. I didn't expect to see you until tomorrow."

"Yeah," he muttered, stepping past her to enter the suite. "Something's come up."

She frowned as he walked into the room, careful not to get close enough to brush against her. Alex noticed that his features were grim, his cheeks shadowed by beard stubble and his hair looked as if he'd been running his fingers through it for hours.

"Garrett? Is something wrong?"

He laughed shortly and turned to look at her. His eyes were dark and filled with charged emotions too deep to name. Shoving his hands into the back pockets of his worn jeans, he just looked at her for a long minute before saying, "Just came to tell you something. You win."

"What?"

Shaking his head, he blew out a breath and said, "I talked to your father a while ago. Told him I quit."

"You did?" All right, she should be pleased, and yet, the look on his face told her that more was coming and that she wasn't going to like it.

"Told him I couldn't take money from him for keeping you safe."

She took a single step toward him. "Why, Garrett? Why would you do that?"

"You know why." His gaze swept her up and down before settling on her eyes again. "But that doesn't mean I'm backing off, Alex. I'm still going to be there. Every day. Making sure nothing happens to you."

"Garrett." She reached up and cupped his cheek in her palm. "Nothing's going to happen to me."

He caught her hand in his and held on. His shadow-filled eyes locked with hers and flashed with steely determination. "Damn straight, it's not."

Her hand trapped in his tight grip, she could only stare up at him. "Garrett, you're even more crazed about protecting me than the palace guards. Why?"

"Because I won't fail again."

"Fail? Fail how?"

He released her, turned and walked to the couch and looked down at the book, spine up on the cushions. He snorted. "Romance novel?"

"There's nothing wrong with a happy ending," she said.

"Happy endings are fictional, Alex."

"They don't have to be."

He turned back to face her. "You don't get it." A choked off laugh shot from his throat. "No reason why you should."

Alex was standing not two feet from him and yet she felt distance stretching out between them. The pale light of her reading lamp was a golden circle in the darkness, reaching for Garrett and not quite making it. Absently she noted the soft roar of the ocean, like an extra heartbeat in the room.

"Then explain it to me, Garrett. Tell me what's driving you."

He reached up, scraped both palms across his face and then shoved them through his hair. When he'd finished, he looked at her and his eyes were bleak, sending a thread of worry sliding through Alex's body.

When he spoke, his voice was rough and low, as if he regretted saying the words even before they were out of his mouth. "About ten years ago, I was hired to be a body-guard for the daughter of a very wealthy man."

Alex held her breath and stayed perfectly still. Finally, she was going to get to the heart of the problem and she didn't want to risk interrupting him. Yet at the same time, she couldn't fight the notion that once he said what he had to, nothing would be the same. For either of them.

"Her name was Kara." A smile briefly twisted his mouth and was gone again in a blink. "She was beautiful and stubborn and smart. A lot like you, really."

A trickle of cold began to snake down her spine and still, she remained quiet.

"I got…distracted," he said and once again shoved a hand through his hair as if somehow he could wipe away the memories swarming in his mind. "I fell in love with her—"

Pain was swift and sharp. Jealousy dug its talons into her heart and twisted. And just as quickly, it all faded away. He had loved, but it was ten years ago and obviously it hadn't ended well. She forced herself to ask, "What happened?"

"I quit my job," he said, and swept the room with his troubled gaze before looking back at her. "Knew I couldn't protect Kara with my focus splintered. Told her father I wouldn't be responsible for her life anymore and I left. Two days later, Kara ditched her new guard and ran away. The letter she left behind said she was running to me. She never got there. She was kidnapped and killed."

"God, Garrett…"

"I won't let that happen to you."

Sympathy briefly warred with frustration inside her. Frustration won. "What makes you think it would? One tragedy doesn't always signal another."

"I know. But even getting past that, it's not just Kara. It's you and me. We're too different, Alex. Our worlds are light years apart." He shook his head and she felt the finality of that one single action. His features were tight, implacable. His voice a promise as he added, "I'm not looking to fall in love, Alex. What would be the point?"

Her heart gave a sudden lurch in her chest, and it felt as if a ball of lead had dropped into the pit of her stomach. He was walking away from her. Without even trying. Without a backward glance. Tears filled her eyes but she furiously blinked them back. She wasn't about to let him see her *cry*. What would be the point anyway?

Whatever she had convinced herself they shared, in reality, it was no more than a holiday fling. A summer romance doomed to die at the end of the season. She loved a man determined to not love her back, and there didn't seem to be a thing she could do to change it.

And would she if she could?

She had her pride after all. And that emotion was leading the charge when she snapped, "I never said anything about love, Garrett."

"Please." He gave her a patient, tired smile that made her want to kick something. "I can see it in your face, feel it in your touch. Alex, you're looking for something I can't give you."

She felt the sting of those words, and actually swayed in place when they hit her. But she kept her chin lifted and her eyes defiant as she corrected, "Not can't. *Won't*."

"Same thing," he said, folding his arms across his chest and glaring down at her.

"For a man who prides himself on seeing every possible angle of every possible situation, you're surprisingly blind."

"Is that right?"

"It is," she answered and took a step closer to him. Her gaze fixed with his. "This isn't even about *me,* Garrett. It's about you and how you look at your life. I'm sorry about Kara. But that wasn't your fault. Bad things happen. You can't stop them. You can only live your life in spite of them."

"She left her guards because of me," he told her flatly. "If I hadn't gotten involved with her, she'd be alive today."

"You don't know that," she told him and saw denial in his eyes. "You're not God, Garrett. You don't have the power of life and death, and you can't personally protect everyone you care about."

"But I can limit those I care about," he said softly.

"So rather than love and risk the pain of losing it, you would make your own world smaller so maybe danger won't notice you? Maybe your circle of loved ones will be tiny enough that nothing bad will touch you?"

He didn't say anything to that, but then, he didn't have to. Alex knew now for certain that what they had was over. He could stay and watch over her as he'd said he would, but there would be no more lovemaking. No more flirtatious fun. No more laughter. There would be only Garrett, in his role of knight errant ready to do battle in defense of his charge.

And that wasn't enough for Alex. Not nearly enough.

Sadly, she shook her head and said, "The difference between you and me is, I won't deny myself something wonderful for fear of losing it."

"That's because you've never lost."

"Wrong again," she said, a half smile curving her mouth. "I just did."

"Alex—"

"I think you should go," she said, though the words tore at her.

This was over. He couldn't have made himself plainer. He didn't want her—he saw her only as his responsibility—and she wanted the magic.

The gulf lying between them was wider than ever.

"Fine. I'll go. But I'll be back in the morning," he said. "Don't leave the hotel without me."

She didn't answer because an order didn't require one. She simply stood, alone in the dim light and listened to the door close behind him.

First thing in the morning, though, the plan changed.

Griffin needed some backup with a client and Garrett had already dumped so much of the company work on his twin lately, he couldn't turn him down. Besides, he figured it might do both he and Alex some good to have some space.

He'd been up half the night, reliving that scene in her penthouse suite. He could still feel the chill in the room when he told her he wouldn't love her. Could still see her eyes when she told him to leave. A low, deep ache settled in his chest, but Garrett accepted it as the price he had to pay for screwing this up so badly.

And he knew that the pain was going to be with him a long, damn time. He was halfway to San Diego when he thought it was late enough that he could call Alex without waking her up. Punching in the phone number, Garrett steered his car down the 405 freeway and waited for what seemed forever for Alex to answer the damn phone. The moment she did, the sound of her voice sent another ping of regret shooting through him.

Mentally, he explained it away. Of course he regretted

that she'd be leaving. Why the hell wouldn't he? He'd spent practically every day with her for more than a week. Why wouldn't he be accustomed to her smile, her laughter? It was only natural that he'd listen for the sound of her accent and get a buzz when he knew he was going to see her.

Didn't mean he cared. Didn't *mean* anything. When she was gone, things would settle down. Get back to normal, he assured himself. Which was all he wanted. The regular world that didn't include runaway princesses.

"Alex, it's me," he said shortly, changing lanes to pass an RV moving at a snail-like speed in the sun-washed morning.

"What is it, Garrett?"

Her voice was clipped now, as if anger was churning just below the surface. He hated to hear it, but it was probably best, he told himself. If she was mad, then she wasn't hurting. He'd never meant to hurt her, God knew. But it had happened anyway and now the best thing he could do was keep up the wall he'd erected between them the night before.

"I won't be able to come over this morning," he said tightly. "Griffin needs some help on a case, and I—"

"No need to explain. I'm sure you're very busy."

The words might be right, but her tone said differently. He scowled at the phone. "Yeah. Well, anyway. You won't be alone. I sent one of our best agents over there. Terri Cooper. She's in the lobby now, waiting for a call from you to the front desk. She's the best in the business, so I know she'll keep you safe."

"Garrett, I don't need a babysitter."

"She's a bodyguard, Alex, and until I get back, she's sticking to you like glue."

"And I've no say in it."

He frowned to himself and downshifted as the flow of

traffic picked up a bit. "If you don't want to see Terri, don't leave the hotel. I'd prefer that anyway. I should be able to be back before dinner."

"I see," she said, her accent a little sharper, "and I'm to await you at your convenience, is that it?"

He punched the accelerator and swung around another car, which had no business driving in the fast lane. "Alex, don't start with me. We've been over this. You know it's not safe."

"No, Garrett," she argued, "*you* know it's not safe. But I've a mind of my own and am in no way burdened with your overwhelmingly cautious nature."

"Damn it, Alex." He thought about hitting the first off-ramp and heading back. Then he realized his twin was in La Jolla waiting for him, and Garrett was stuck between the proverbial rock and a hard place.

And he did *not* have a cautious nature.

Made him sound like some old lady afraid to leave her house. Nothing could be further from the truth. He faced down danger every damn day of his life. It was *Alex* facing danger he couldn't bear the thought of.

"I'm in charge of your safety."

"No, you're not. You said yourself last night that you're no longer working for my father. That makes you nothing more than a bossy ex-bed partner. And I don't take orders from my exes."

"You're making me crazy, Alex. Terri will be with you if you leave the hotel."

Someone cut him off and Garrett honked at them. Didn't do any good, but made him feel a little better.

"I won't promise anything. And if that makes you crazy, then I'll admit to enjoying your misery as a side benefit."

She was enjoying it, too. He heard it in her voice. God knew what she would do today just to prove to him that she could take care of herself. He didn't even want to think about it.

The stream of traffic was slowing down. Brake lights flashed ahead and cars were stacked up behind him, too. Just another day on Southern California's freeways. Once he was stopped dead, he muttered, "I'll be back as soon as I can. Just—be careful, okay?"

There was a long pause and, for a moment, he half wondered if she'd hung up on him and he hadn't noticed. Then finally, she said only, "Goodbye, Garrett."

Car horns blared, the radio in the car beside him was set to a volume probably audible in space and the only sound Garrett really noticed was the hum of the dial tone, telling him she was gone.

"She's making me nuts."

"In her defense," Griffin said helpfully, "she didn't have far to go."

"Thanks for that." Garrett gave his twin a dark look. "You're supposed to be on my side, remember? Blood thicker than water and all that?"

"Yeah, we're family, blah, blah," Griffin said, kicking back in the leather booth seat and pausing long enough to take a long pull on his bottle of beer. "But if the princess is getting to you this badly, then I'm all for it."

Garrett stared down at his own beer and then lifted his gaze to look around the half-empty pub. It was supposed to look Irish, but Garrett had seen the real thing not long ago when he did a job for his cousin Jefferson. Still, it wasn't bad, just touristy. Lots of dark wood, flags of Ireland all over the place and even a bronze leprechaun crouched on the bar.

He and Griffin had finished with their client early and had stopped in here for some lunch before facing the long drive home again. He was still worried about Alex, but she'd been on her own for hours already, doing God knew what—because the damn woman wouldn't answer her damn phone. All Terri sent him was a brief text saying everything was fine. So him taking a half hour for lunch wasn't going to make that much difference at this point.

"And did I mention," Griffin said with a knowing leer, "you look like *hell?*"

He had known that talking to Griffin about all of this wouldn't get him any sympathy. And maybe he didn't need any. What he needed was somebody to talk to.

He should have picked someone smarter.

"Doesn't matter if she's 'getting' to me or not—which she isn't," he added, after a pause for a sip of beer. "The point is she's a princess, Griff. Would never work."

"Man, I really did get all the brains," Griffin mused with a slow shake of his head. "The way you talk about her, she seems damn near perfect. And you don't want her because she's a princess? What is that?"

"It's not a question of want."

"Then what is it?"

"Even if I did admit to wanting Alex, the fact that she's a princess pretty much cools that whole idea."

"Because..."

Irritated, Garrett glared at his twin. "You think her family would want her with a security expert?"

"Who better?"

"Nice try. But royals prefer royals, and everyone knows that. Her father's probably got her future husband all picked out for her." The thought of that made him want to break something.

"Uh-huh. And what else?" Griffin shook his head. "There's more here, Garrett."

"Kara." He'd loved once and lost her. He wasn't sure he was willing to go through that again.

"Here we go," Griffin muttered. "You know, I've been hearing that excuse for years, and I'm just not buying it anymore."

"What the hell's that mean?"

"It means, that you've been hiding behind Kara. Yeah, it was terrible what happened to her. But you know damn well it wasn't your fault."

Garrett shifted in his seat, took a swig of beer and set the bottle down again.

"You loved her, and she died."

"Thanks for the news flash. But I don't need you to tell me that. I lived it."

Griffin ignored him. Leaning on the tabletop, he said, "Somewhere along the way, though, you died, too. Or at least you stopped living, which amounts to the same thing."

Garrett glared at his twin again, but it didn't do any good. Nothing could shut Griffin up if he had something to say and clearly he did. Seemed he'd been building up to this little speech for years.

"Now along comes the princess, shakes you up, makes you notice, *hey, not a bad world out here,* and *boom.*" He clapped both hands together for emphasis. "You shut down. Start pulling Kara out of the past and using her as a shield or some damn thing. The problem isn't Kara, Garrett. Never was. The problem is *you.*"

The waitress arrived with their lunch and while Griffin flirted and got an extra order of fries for his trouble, Garrett did some fast thinking. His twin might actually have a point. He had been enjoying his time with Alex. Had been relaxing the guard around his heart and the minute she got close, he'd pulled back. So was he using Kara as a shield? If that was true, then Alex had been right the night before when she'd accused him of making sure his world was small enough that tragedy would have a harder time striking.

When it was just the two of them again, Griffin noted, "Hmm. Looks like a lightbulb might have gone off in your head."

"Maybe," Garrett admitted, then added, "but even if you're right—"

"Can't hear that often enough," Griffin said with a grin just before popping a French fry into his mouth.

"—it doesn't change the fact that Alex is a princess and lives in a palace for God's sake. I live in a condo at the beach—"

"No, you don't," Griffin interrupted.

"Excuse me?" Seriously, he knew where he *lived.*

Taking another pull of his beer, Griffin said, "You don't live there. You live out of suitcases. Hell, you spend more time on King Jets than you do in that condo."

"What's that supposed to mean?"

"Means you don't live anywhere, Garrett. So what's keeping you here?"

He just stared at his twin. Was he the only one who could see the problems in this? Alex was oblivious and now Griffin, too? "Our *business?*"

"More excuses." Griff waved one hand at his brother, effectively dismissing him, then picked up his burger and took a bite. After chewing, he said, "We can run our place from anywhere. If you wanted to, you could set up a European branch and you damn well know it."

His chest felt tight. The noise in the pub fell away. All he could hear was himself, telling Alex that he wouldn't love her. That he couldn't. The problem was, he *did* love her.

A hell of a thing for a man to just be figuring out. But

there it was. He'd had to quit working for her father because he couldn't take money for protecting the woman he loved. He had kept his distance from her because he couldn't sleep with her knowing that he'd have to let her go.

But did he have to?

What if he was wrong? What if there was a chance a commoner might have a shot with a princess? Was he really ready to let Alex go without even *trying* to make it work? His brain raced with possibilities. Maybe he had been short-sighted. Stupid. But he didn't have to stay that way.

His phone rang, and he glanced at the readout. Instantly, he answered it and fought the sudden hot ball of worry in his guts. "Terri? What is it?"

"Boss, I'm sorry, but you *did* tell me to stick to her and—"

"What happened?" In his mind, he was seeing car wrecks, holdups, assassins...

"She had me drive her to L.A. and—"

"Uh, Garrett..."

"Shut up," he muttered, then to Terri he said, "L.A.? Why L.A.?"

"Garrett!"

His gaze snapped to Griffin.

Pointing to the bar, his twin said, "You need to see this."

He turned to look. Terri was still talking in his ear, but he hardly heard her. There was a flat screen TV above the bar, the sound muted. But he didn't need the sound. What he saw opened a hole in his chest. He snapped the phone shut and stared.

Alex was on the TV. But an Alex he hardly knew. Her long, thick hair was twisted into a complicated knot at the top of her head. Diamonds winked at her ears and blazed at the base of her throat. She wore a pale green dress that was tailored to fit her beautifully and she looked as remote as a…well, a *princess*.

Garrett pushed out of his seat, crossed the room and ordered the bartender to, "Turn it up, will you?"

The man did and Garrett listened over the roaring in his own ears. Someone shoved a microphone at Alex and shouted, "Princess, how long have you been here and why the big secret?"

She smiled into the camera, and Garrett could have sworn she was looking directly at him. His hands curled around the edge of the polished wood bar and squeezed until he was half afraid he was going to snap the thick wood in two.

"I've been in America almost two weeks," she said, her voice low, moderate, regal. "As for the secrecy of my visit, I wanted the opportunity to see the *real* America. To meet people and get to know them without the barriers of my name and background getting in the way."

People in the bar were listening. Griffin had moved up alongside him, but Garrett hardly noticed. His gaze was fixed on Alex. She looked so different. And already so far away.

"Did it work?" someone else shouted.

"It did," she said, her gaze still steady on the camera, staring directly into Garrett's soul. "I've enjoyed myself immensely. This is a wonderful country, and I've been met with nothing but kindness and warmth."

"You're headed home now, Princess," a reporter called out. "What're you going to miss the most?"

There was a long, thoughtful pause before Alex smiled into the camera and said, "It's a difficult question. I loved Disneyland, of course. And the beach. But I think what

I loved most were the people I met. *They* are what I'll miss when I go home. *They* are what will stay with me. Always."

She was leaving.

And maybe, he told himself darkly, it was better this way. But even he didn't believe that.

The camera pulled away and an excited news anchor came on to say, "Princess Alexis of Cadria, speaking to you from the Cadrian Consulate in Los Angeles. I can tell you we were all surprised to get the notice of her brief press conference. Speculation will be rife now, as to just where the princess has been for the last week or more.

"But this afternoon, a private jet will be taking her back to her home country. A shame we didn't get to see more of the lovely Princess Alexis while she was here."

Garrett had already turned away when the woman shifted gears and launched into another story. Walking back to their booth, Garrett sat down, picked up his burger and methodically took a bite. There was no reason to hurry through lunch now.

"Garrett—"

He glared his twin into silence and concentrated on the burger that suddenly tasted like sawdust.

Twelve

Everything was just as she'd left it.

Why that should have surprised Alex, she couldn't have said. But it did. Somehow, she felt so...changed, that she had expected to find the palace different as well.

Standing on the stone terrace outside the morning room, she turned to look up at the pink stone walls of the palace she called home. The leaded glass windows winked in the early morning sunlight and the flag of Cadria, flying high atop the far turret, snapped in the breeze.

She was both comforted and irritated that life in Cadria had marched inexorably on while she had been gone. But then, her emotions were swinging so wildly lately, that didn't surprise her, either. Since coming home a week ago, she had slipped seamlessly back into the life she had so briefly left behind. She had already visited two schools and presided over the planting of new trees in the city's park.

The papers were still talking about her spontaneous visit to the U.S. and photographers still haunted her every step.

Now, when she wanted to go shopping, she couldn't just walk to the closest mall or wander down to the neighborhood shops. A shopping excursion became more of a battle strategy. There were guards, which she told herself, Garrett would thoroughly approve of, there were state cars and flags flying from the bumpers. There were stores closed to all other shoppers and bowing deference from shopkeepers.

God, how she missed being a nobody.

Of course, her family didn't see it that way. They were all delighted to have her back. Her oldest brother was about to become engaged, and the other two were doing what they did best. Immersing themselves in royal duties with the occasional break for polo or auto racing. Her parents were the same, though her father hadn't yet interrogated her about her holiday and Alex suspected she had her mother to thank for that.

And she appreciated the reprieve. She just wasn't ready to talk about Garrett yet. Not to anybody. She was still hoping to somehow wipe him out of her mind. What was the point in torturing herself forever over a man who saw her as nothing more than an anvil around his neck?

"Bloody idiot," she muttered and kicked the stone barrier hard enough to send a jolt of pain through her foot and up her leg. But at least it was *physical* pain, which was a lot easier to deal with.

"Well," a familiar voice said from behind her, "that's more like it."

Alex looked over her shoulder at her mother. Queen Teresa of Cadria was still beautiful. Tall and elegant, Alex's mother kept her graying blond hair in a short cut that swung along her jawline. She wore green slacks, a white silk blouse and taupe flats. Her only jewelry was her wedding ring. Her blue eyes were sharp and fixed on her daughter.

"Mom. I didn't know you were there."

"Clearly," Teresa said as she strolled casually across the terrace, "care to tell me who the 'bloody idiot' is? Or will you make me guess?"

The queen calmly hitched herself up to sit on the stone parapet and demurely crossed her feet at the ankles. Alex couldn't help but smile. In public, Teresa of Cadria was dignified, elegant and all things proper. But when the family was alone, she became simply Teresa Hawkins Wells. A California girl who had married a king.

She had bowed to some traditions and had livened up other staid areas of the palace with her more casual flair. For instance, when she became queen, Teresa had made it clear that the "old" way of raising royal children wouldn't be happening anymore. She had been a hands-on mother and had remained that way. Naturally, there had also been governesses and tutors, but Alex and her brothers had grown up knowing their parents' love—and there were many royals who couldn't claim that.

None of Teresa's children had ever been able to keep a secret from her for long. And not one of them had ever successfully lied to their mother. So Alex didn't even bother trying now.

"Garrett King," she said.

"As I suspected." Teresa smiled as encouragement.

Alex didn't need much. Strange, she hadn't thought she wanted to talk about him, yet now that the opportunity was here, she found the words couldn't come fast enough. "He's arrogant and pompous and bossy. Always ordering me about, as bad as Dad, really. But he made me laugh as often as he made me angry and—"

"You love him," her mother finished for her.

"Yes, but I'll get over it," Alex said with determination.

"Why would you want to?"

The first sting of tears hit her eyes and that only made Alex more furious. She swiped at them with impatient fingers and said, "Because he doesn't want me." She shook her head and looked away from her mom's sympathetic eyes to stare out over the palace's formal gardens.

She focused on the box hedge maze. The maze had been constructed more than three hundred years ago, and Alex smiled, remembering how she and her brothers used to run through its long, twisting patterns at night, trying to scare each other.

The maze was so famous it was one of the most popular parts of the castle tour that was offered every summer. But the most beautiful part of the garden was the roses. They were Alex's mother's pride and joy. Teresa had brought slips of California roses with her when she'd given up her life to be queen. And she still nurtured those plants herself, despite grumblings from the head gardener.

Their thick scent wafted to them now, and Alex took a deep breath, letting the familiar become a salve to her wounded pride.

"Alex," her mother said, reaching out to lay one hand on her daughter's arm, "of course he wants you. Why else would he refuse to take money for protecting you?"

"Stubbornness?" Alex asked, shifting her gaze to her mother.

Teresa smiled and shook her head. "Now who's being stubborn?"

"You don't understand, Mom." Alex turned her back on

the garden and pushed herself up to sit beside her mother. The damp cold from the stones leached into her black slacks and slid into her bones, but she hardly noticed. "It was different for you. You met Dad at Disneyland, and it was magic. He fell in love and swept you off your feet and—"

She stopped and stared when her mother's laughter rang out around her. "What's so funny?"

"Oh, sweetie," Teresa said as she caught her breath again. "I didn't mean to laugh, but...maybe your father was right. When you were a little girl, he used to tell me I was spinning too many romantic stories. Filling your head with impossible expectations."

Confused, Alex just looked at her mother. "But you did meet at Disneyland. And you fell in love and became a queen."

"All true," her mother said, "but, that's not *all* of the story."

Intrigued, Alex let her own troubles move to the background as she listened to her mother.

"I did meet Gregory at Disneyland," she said, a half smile on her face. "I was working at the Emporium and he came in and bought half the merchandise at my station just so he'd have an excuse to keep standing there talking to me."

Alex could enjoy the story even more now that she had been to the famous park and could imagine the scene more clearly.

"We spent a lot of time together in the two weeks he was in California and, long story short, we fell in love." She smiled again, then picked up Alex's hand and gave it a squeeze. "But it wasn't happily ever after right away, sweetie."

"What happened?"

"Your dad left. He came back here, to the palace." She swept her gaze up to take in the pink castle and its centuries of tradition. "He told me he was going to be a king and that he couldn't marry me. That we couldn't possibly be together. His parents wouldn't have allowed it, and his country wouldn't stand for it."

"What? That's ridiculous!" Alex immediately defended her. "Cadria *loves* you."

"Yes," her mother said with a laugh. "*Now.* Back then, though, it was a different story. I was heartbroken and furious that he would walk away from love so easily."

She and her mother had more in common than Alex knew, she thought glumly. But at least her mom had eventually gotten a happy ending. But how? "What happened?"

"Your father missed me," Teresa said with a grin. "He called, but I wouldn't speak to him. He sent me gifts that I returned. Letters that went back unopened." Nudging Alex's shoulder with her own, Teresa admitted, "I drove him crazy."

"Good for you. I can't believe Dad walked away from you!"

"Centuries of tradition are hard to fight," Teresa said. "And so was your grandfather who had no interest in a commoner daughter-in-law."

"But—"

"I know, sweetie. Your grandfather loved me. Once he met me, everything was fine." She sighed a little. "But, your dad actually had to threaten to abdicate before his father would listen to reason."

"Dad was willing to give up the throne for you?"

"He was," Teresa said with another sigh of satisfaction. "Thankfully, it didn't come to that, since he's a very good king. But once his father saw how serious Gregory was, he promised to make it work. He went to the Law Chambers himself to see that the country's charter was rewritten to allow for a commoner as queen."

"Wow." She didn't know what else to say. Alex had had no idea of the intrigue and passion and clashes that had been involved in her parents getting together.

"Yes, wow," Teresa said, laughing again. "When it was all settled, in a record amount of time, thanks to your father being an impatient soul, Gregory came back to California with his grandmother's ring in hand and the rest, as they say, is history."

Holding up her left hand as proof, Teresa wiggled her fingers, letting the ancient diamond wink and glitter in the sunlight.

"I had no idea."

"Of course you didn't, and I should have told you the whole truth sooner. But, Alex, I had a point in telling you this now," her mother said and reached out to give her a one-armed hug. "And that is, don't give up on your young man. Love is a powerful thing and, once felt, it's impossible to walk away from. If your Garrett is anything like my Gregory..." She smiled again. "There's always hope."

"Excuse me, your majesty."

Teresa looked to the open doorway into the morning room. A maid stood in the shadows. "Yes, Christa?"

"I've laid the tea out, ma'am, for you and her highness."

"Thank you, Christa," Teresa said, "we'll be right in."

A quick curtsy and the maid was gone again. A moment later, Teresa scooted off the parapet, dusted off the seat of her slacks and said, "I'll pour the tea. You come in when you're ready, okay?"

Nodding, Alex watched her mother go, as her mind

whirled with possibilities. Was her mom right? Was there hope? Yes, her parents' love story had turned out well in the end, but the King of Cadria had been in love.

Whereas Garrett King *refused* to be in love with her.

She turned her head to stare out over the gardens, to the ocean beyond and to the man on the other side of the world. Hope, she thought wistfully, could be a both a blessing and a curse.

"She sent it back."

"What?" Griffin looked up as Garrett stormed into his office.

Tossing a small package onto his brother's desk, Garrett complained, "The necklace I sent to Alex two days ago. She returned it!"

"And this is my problem because…"

"You're my brother, and it's your job to listen to me," Garrett told him as he stalked the perimeter of his brother's office.

"Actually, it's my job to look into the file we just got on our Georgia client and—"

"Why would she return it?" Garrett asked no one in particular, thinking of the platinum and onyx piece he'd had commissioned just for her. He hadn't asked himself why it was so important for him to give her a memento of their time together. It simply was. He couldn't have her, but damned if he could entirely let go, either.

These past two weeks without her had nearly killed him. Nothing felt right to him anymore. Without Alex in his life, everything else was just white noise. He kept as busy as possible and *still* her absence chewed at him, widening the black hole inside him every damn day.

His fingers closed around the box that had been returned to him just a few minutes ago. Shaking it for emphasis, he blurted, "It was a trinket. Sort of a souvenir. You know, help her remember her holiday."

Griffin gave up and sat back in his chair. "Maybe she doesn't *want* to remember."

Garrett stopped dead and glared at his twin. "Why the hell wouldn't she want to remember? She had a great time."

"Yeah, but it's over, and she's back home at the palace."

"So, close the door? That's it?" Could she really cut him out of her life, her memories, that easily?

"Aren't you the one who closed the door?" Griffin asked.

"Not the point." Hell, Garrett knew he wasn't making any sense. He didn't need his twin stating the obvious.

Two weeks without her. Didn't seem to matter that he knew he'd done the right thing. Didn't matter that he knew there was no way they could have worked out anything between them. He missed her like he would an arm. Or a leg.

She was as much a part of him as his damn heart and without her, it was like he didn't have one.

This had not been a part of the plan. He'd expected to miss her, sure. But he hadn't counted on not being able to sleep or keep his mind on his damn work. He hadn't counted on seeing her everywhere, hearing her voice, her laugh in his mind at odd moments during the day.

"You're just going to prowl around my office, is that it?" Griffin asked.

Garrett stopped and glared at him. "What the hell am I supposed to do?"

"You know what I think you should do. Question is, what are you *going* to do?"

"If I knew that," he muttered darkly, "I'd be doing it."

"Well then, maybe this will help you decide," Griffin said and pulled the morning paper out from under a stack of files. "Wasn't going to show you this—but maybe you should see it after all."

"What?" Garrett took the paper, glanced at the picture on the front page and felt his heart stop.

Front and center, there was a photo of Alex, dressed in a flowing gown and a crown, holding on to the arm of an impossibly handsome man in a tux, wearing a damn sash across his chest that was loaded down with medals. The tagline above the photo screamed, Royal Engagement In The Wind?

"Oh, *hell* no," Garrett muttered.

"Looks to me like you'd better go get your woman back before it's too late," Griffin said, clearly amused at Garrett's reaction.

Garrett's vision fogged at the edges until all he could see was Alex's face staring up at him from the paper. He was about to really lose her. Permanently. Unless he took a chance.

Clutching the newspaper tight in one fist, Garrett grabbed the returned package and said, "Call the airport for me. Have one of the King Jets fueled up and ready to go when I get there."

Griffin was laughing as he made the call, but Garrett was already gone.

"Where is he?" Garrett stormed past the footman at the door to the castle and stomped loudly across the marble flooring. His head turned as if on a swivel as he scanned every hallway for signs of the king.

"If you'll follow me," the butler said, "his majesty is in the library."

Garrett hadn't slept in nearly twenty-four hours. He felt ragged and pushed to the edge of his endurance, but damned if he was going to wait another minute to talk to Alex's father. He'd gotten past the palace guards on the strength of his having done work for the crown before. But getting an audience with the king this easily was a plus.

The air smelled of roses and beeswax, and Garrett took a deep breath to steady himself for the coming confrontation. The sound of his footsteps as he followed after his guide rang out hollowly in the air, thudding like a heartbeat. He had a plan, of course. Wasn't much of one, but he'd use whatever he could. Alex was here, somewhere, and no matter what happened between him and the king in the next few minutes, he wasn't leaving until he spoke to her.

He stepped into the library and the butler left him with the king. The room was imposing, as it was meant to be. Dark paneling, bloodred leather furniture and floor-to-ceiling windows with a view of the sea. The man standing before a crackling fire was just as imposing. King Gregory was tall, muscular and the gray in his hair only made him look more formidable.

"Garrett, this is a surprise."

About to be an even bigger one, he thought and cut right to the chase. "Your majesty, Alex can't marry Duke Henrik."

"Is that right?" One eyebrow lifted.

Hell, Garrett couldn't believe the man would allow Alex *near* the duke. A quick online search had been enough to show Garrett that the man was more known for his string of women than for any work done in the House of Lords.

Well, the king might be okay with that, but damned if Garrett would let Alex end up with someone who didn't deserve her.

"How is this any of your business, Garrett?"

"It's my business because there's a good chance Alex is pregnant with my child."

Risky move, he told himself, since there was no way Alex was pregnant. But it was the one sure way he knew to delay any kind of wedding but for the one Garrett now wanted more than anything.

The king's face went red. "You—"

"Pregnant?"

Garrett whirled around at the deep voice behind him and was just in time to watch Alex's older brother Prince Christopher's fist collide with his face. Pain exploded inside his head, but he ducked before the prince could land another one.

Then he threw a fast right himself and watched the prince stagger backward. The other man recovered quickly and came at Garrett again, still furious.

The king was shouting, "Pregnant? *Pregnant?*"

Two more men ran into the room. They took in the scene at a glance and immediately joined their older brother in the fray.

"Perfect," Garrett muttered, turning a slow circle so he could keep an eye on all three of them. Seemed he wasn't going to come out of this without a few bruises. But he'd give as good as he got, too.

He blocked another blow, threw a punch himself and smiled when the youngest of the princes was laid out flat on his back. The king pushed past one of his sons and threw a punch of his own that Garrett managed to avoid.

He wasn't about to hit a king, either, so he focused on protecting himself and doing a lot of dodging.

As Garrett avoided another blow, he yelled, "Just let me talk to Alex and we can straighten this out."

"You stay away from my sister." This from the prince pushing up from the floor.

"No one is talking to anyone until I have some answers," the king shouted again.

"Why is everyone yelling?" Alex called into the mix.

Garrett turned at the sound of her voice and Christopher landed another solid jab on his jaw. "Damn it!"

Hands clapped loudly, followed by a sharp, feminine command. "Stop this at once! Christopher, no more fighting. Help Henry off the floor, and Jonathon, get your father some water."

The king was sputtering in rage, but everyone else moved to follow the queen's orders. Everyone but Alex. She just stood there in the doorway, staring at him as if she'd never seen him before. Her hair was tidy, her elegant dress and tasteful jewelry made her seem unapproachable. But somewhere beneath that cool exterior was *his* Alex. And Garrett wasn't leaving until he'd had a chance to reach her.

The capper for Garrett, though, was seeing the damn duke standing right behind her. That settled everything. No way in hell was Garrett letting his woman go. And she *was* his. Had been from that first day at Disneyland.

"Who's pregnant?" Alex demanded.

"Apparently, *you* are," Christopher told her.

"I'm *what?*" She fired a furious look on Garrett and he just glared right back.

"I said you could be."

"Pregnant?" Henrik repeated from behind her. "You're *pregnant?* I'll be leaving."

"Henrik!" The king's shout went unanswered as the duke scuttled out the door to disappear. Probably forever.

"What is going on here? I could hear the shouts all the way to the garden." The queen looked from one face to the next, her silent, accusatory stare demanding answers.

"Garrett King claims Alexis is pregnant with his child," the king managed to say through gritted teeth.

"And I was just about to beat him to a pulp," Christopher said helpfully.

"In your dreams," Garrett muttered, never taking his eyes off Alex.

"Well, it's a lie," she snapped. "I'm not pregnant."

No one was listening. The princes were arguing among themselves, the queen and the king were locked into battle and Alex was looking at Garrett through furious eyes. When she turned to leave, he bolted across the room, grabbed her hand and tugged her into the hall, away from her arguing family.

"Don't," she said, pulling her hand free. Looking up at him, she said, "You don't belong here, Garrett. Go home."

"No."

"You had your choice, and you made it. Now it's time we both live with it."

He grabbed her again, holding on to her shoulders half worried that she'd run if he let her go. It could take him *weeks* to find her again in this place. "Why did you return the package I sent you?"

"Because what we had is over. Now please, just *go.*"

"I'm not going anywhere," he murmured and pulled her in close. Wrapping his arms around her, to hold on tight when she started to squirm, Garrett kissed her. He poured everything he'd been feeling for the last two weeks into that kiss. The longing. The pain. The regret. The joy at being with her again. For the first time in too damn long, he felt whole. As if the puzzle pieces of his life had fallen into place.

Her tongue tangled with his, her breath slid into his lungs and her heartbeat clamored in time with his own. Everything was right. He just had to convince her that he was a changed man.

Finally, he broke the kiss, stared down into those amazing eyes of hers and said, "Alex, I don't give a damn about your crown. I don't care that you're a princess. Don't care that our worlds are so different. I'll convince your father to let us be together. We can make it work, Alex. We *will* make it work."

"Garrett…" She sighed, and said, "I want to believe you. But you made yourself perfectly clear before. You didn't want me in California. So why now? What's changed?"

"Me," he told her, lifting his hands to cup her face. His thumbs moved over her cheekbones and just the feel of her soft, smooth skin beneath his eased the pain that had been tearing at him for what seemed forever. "I've changed. And I did want you in California, Alex. I always wanted you. From the first time I saw you in Disneyland, I wanted you. I was just too busy looking for trouble to see what I'd already found."

She shook her head, and Garrett's heart stopped briefly. But a King never backed away from a challenge. Especially one that meant more to him than his life.

"Alex, I know now what's really important." God, he had to make her believe him. Those eyes of hers were so deep, so rich with emotion, with *love.* Seeing it gave him enough hope to continue. To tell her everything he wanted her to know.

And he still hadn't even said the most important thing. "I love you. I *love* you, Alex, Princess Alexis Morgan Wells. I really do."

Her breath caught and a single tear rolled from the corner of her eye. He caught it with his thumb as if it were precious. Sunlight speared in from an overhead window and lay on her beautiful hair, now tightly controlled in a twist on top of her head.

"I love your laugh." His gaze moved over her and then he reached up to tug a few pins loose, letting her hair fall down around her shoulders. "And I love your hair, all wild and tangled. I love the way you find something beautiful in everything. I love your clever brain and your smart-ass mouth. I love that you're willing to call me out when you think I'm being an idiot."

Her lips quirked.

"And I love that you want to help women in need and I'd like to be a part of that."

She took a sharp breath.

"I want to be with you, Alex. Always. I want to build a life with you. In California *and* Cadria."

"How—"

"I'm opening a branch of King Security right here in Cadria. We'll be the European division."

"Garrett—" She shook her head sadly. "You're not used to this kind of life. I'm followed by reporters and photographers. We wouldn't be able to just buy a house in town and move in. We would have to live here in a wing of the palace. You'd hate that, you know you would."

He laughed shortly. "First off, you forget. I'm one of the Kings of California. We've got paparazzi following us all the damn time looking for a story. I'm used to life in a fishbowl. It's not always pretty, but if you want to badly enough, you can carve out a private life."

"But—"

"And it doesn't matter where we live, Alex," he said, "as long as we're together." He gave a glance around the wide hallway, with its priceless art hanging on the walls and the gleam of marble shining up at them. "I could learn to love the palace."

She laughed, and God, it sounded like music to him.

"I'll miss good Thai food at one in the morning, but if the craving gets bad, I'll have Griffin send me some on a King Jet."

"Oh, Garrett," she said on a chuckle.

"It'll work, Princess," he said quickly, giving her a quick kiss as if to seal a promise. "We'll blend our lives and build one together that will suit both of us."

Alex's breath caught in her chest. Everything she had ever dreamed of was right here, in front of her. All she had to do was reach out and take it. Returning the package he had sent her hadn't been easy, but she'd hoped that he would come to her, repeating family history. Now, here he was and Alex was half afraid to believe in it.

"I love you, Alex," he said softly. "Marry me. Love me back."

She sighed and lifted both arms to wrap them around his neck. "I do love you, Garrett King."

"Thank God," he said on a laugh, dropping his forehead to hers. "When you returned the necklace…"

"It was a necklace?"

"I brought it with me." He dipped one hand into his pocket and pulled out a flat, dark green jeweler's box.

Alex took it, opened the lid and sighed with pleasure.

"It's a seagull," he told her unnecessarily. "I had it made to remind you of the ocean. Of all the time we spent at the beach."

Tears stung her eyes as she lifted the beautifully crafted piece free of the box. She turned and lifted her hair so that he could put it around her neck and when it was lying against the base of her throat, she touched it and whispered, "I love it, Garrett, though I don't need a reminder. I'll never forget a moment of my time with you."

She had everything she had ever dreamed of, right there in her arms. Garrett King was looking at her with more love than she could have imagined possible. She felt the truth of it in his touch. Saw it plainly in his beautiful eyes that were no longer shadowed with old pain. Her heart felt full and yet...

"I'm still a princess, Garrett," she warned. "That won't change, ever. There will still be the chance of danger surrounding me and my family. It will still drive you crazy."

"Yeah," he said solemnly. "I know. But I'll be here to make sure you're safe. All of you." A small smile crooked one corner of his mouth. "King Security can be the palace's personal protection detail.

"Marry me, Alex. Together, you and I can do anything."

"I know we can," she said and went up on her toes to kiss him. "So yes, Garrett, I'll marry you."

He grinned and blew out a relieved breath. "Took you long enough."

Shaking her head, she said, "I can't believe you told my father I was pregnant."

"It was the only thing I could come up with on short notice."

She smiled up at him. "You used to be a much better liar, Mr. King."

"It's all in the past, Princess. No more lies. Not between us."

"Agreed," she said, a grin she felt might never go away curving her mouth.

"So," he asked as he leaned in to kiss her, "how do you feel about Disneyland for a honeymoon?"

"I think that sounds perfect."

Then he kissed her, and the world righted itself again. Alex reveled in the sensation of everything being just as it should be. She gave herself up to the wonder and the joy and wasn't even aware when her brothers and father burst into the hall to see why things had gotten so suddenly quiet.

And she didn't see when her mother ushered her men back into the study to allow her daughter time to enjoy the magic of a lifetime.

* * * * *

PASSION

For a spicier, decidedly hotter read—
this is your destination for romance!

COMING NEXT MONTH
AVAILABLE MARCH 13, 2012

#2143 TEMPTED BY HER INNOCENT KISS
Pregnancy & Passion
Maya Banks

#2144 BEHIND BOARDROOM DOORS
Dynasties: The Kincaids
Jennifer Lewis

#2145 THE PATERNITY PROPOSITION
Billionaires and Babies
Merline Lovelace

#2146 A TOUCH OF PERSUASION
The Men of Wolff Mountain
Janice Maynard

#2147 A FORBIDDEN AFFAIR
The Master Vintners
Yvonne Lindsay

#2148 CAUGHT IN THE SPOTLIGHT
Jules Bennett

REQUEST YOUR FREE BOOKS!
2 FREE NOVELS PLUS 2 FREE GIFTS!

Harlequin

Desire

ALWAYS POWERFUL, PASSIONATE AND PROVOCATIVE

YES! Please send me 2 FREE Harlequin Desire® novels and my 2 FREE gifts (gifts are worth about $10). After receiving them, if I don't wish to receive any more books, I can return the shipping statement marked "cancel." If I don't cancel, I will receive 6 brand-new novels every month and be billed just $4.30 per book in the U.S. or $4.99 per book in Canada. That's a saving of at least 14% off the cover price! It's quite a bargain! Shipping and handling is just 50¢ per book in the U.S. and 75¢ per book in Canada.* I understand that accepting the 2 free books and gifts places me under no obligation to buy anything. I can always return a shipment and cancel at any time. Even if I never buy another book, the two free books and gifts are mine to keep forever.

225/326 HDN FEF3

_____

Name   (PLEASE PRINT)

_____

Address   Apt. #

_____

City   State/Prov.   Zip/Postal Code

_____

Signature (if under 18, a parent or guardian must sign)

Mail to the **Reader Service:**

IN U.S.A.: P.O. Box 1867, Buffalo, NY 14240-1867
IN CANADA: P.O. Box 609, Fort Erie, Ontario L2A 5X3

Not valid for current subscribers to Harlequin Desire books.

Want to try two free books from another line?
Call 1-800-873-8635 or visit www.ReaderService.com.

* Terms and prices subject to change without notice. Prices do not include applicable taxes. Sales tax applicable in N.Y. Canadian residents will be charged applicable taxes. Offer not valid in Quebec. This offer is limited to one order per household. All orders subject to credit approval. Credit or debit balances in a customer's account(s) may be offset by any other outstanding balance owed by or to the customer. Please allow 4 to 6 weeks for delivery. Offer available while quantities last.

Your Privacy—The Reader Service is committed to protecting your privacy. Our Privacy Policy is available online at www.ReaderService.com or upon request from the Reader Service.

We make a portion of our mailing list available to reputable third parties that offer products we believe may interest you. If you prefer that we not exchange your name with third parties, or if you wish to clarify or modify your communication preferences, please visit us at www.ReaderService.com/consumerschoice or write to us at Reader Service Preference Service, P.O. Box 9062, Buffalo, NY 14269. Include your complete name and address.

HDES11B

New York Times *and* USA TODAY *bestselling author Maya Banks presents book three in her miniseries* PREGNANCY & PASSION.

TEMPTED BY HER INNOCENT KISS

Available March 2012 from Harlequin Desire!

There came a time in a man's life when he knew he was well and truly caught. Devon Carter stared down at the diamond ring nestled in velvet and acknowledged that this was one such time. He snapped the lid closed and shoved the box into the breast pocket of his suit.

He had two choices. He could marry Ashley Copeland and fulfill his goal of merging his company with Copeland Hotels, thus creating the largest, most exclusive line of resorts in the world, or he could refuse and lose it all.

Put in that light, there wasn't much he could do except pop the question.

The doorman to his Manhattan high-rise apartment hurried to open the door as Devon strode toward the street. He took a deep breath before ducking into his car, and the driver pulled into traffic.

Tonight was the night. All of his careful wooing, the countless dinners, kisses that started brief and casual and became more breathless—all a lead-up to tonight. Tonight his seduction of Ashley Copeland would be complete, and then he'd ask her to marry him.

He shook his head as the absurdity of the situation hit him for the hundredth time. Personally, he thought William Copeland was crazy for forcing his daughter down Devon's throat.

Ashley was a sweet enough girl, but Devon had no desire

to marry anyone.

William had other plans. He'd told Devon that Ashley had no head for the family business. She was too softhearted, too naive. So he'd made Ashley part of the deal. The catch? Ashley wasn't to know of it. Which meant Devon was stuck playing stupid games.

Ashley was supposed to think this was a grand love match. She was a starry-eyed woman who preferred her animal-rescue foundation over board meetings, charts and financials for Copeland Hotels.

If she ever found out the truth, she wouldn't take it well.

And hell, he couldn't blame her.

But no matter the reason for his proposal, before the night was over, she'd have no doubts that she belonged to him.

What will happen when Devon marries Ashley?
Find out in Maya Banks's passionate new novel
TEMPTED BY HER INNOCENT KISS
Available March 2012 from Harlequin Desire!

HDEXP0312

USA TODAY bestselling author

Carol Marinelli

begins a daring duet.

THE SECRETS of XANOS

Two brothers alike in charisma and power; separated at birth and seeking revenge...

Nico has always felt like an outsider. He's turned his back on his parents' fortune to become one of Xanos's most powerful exports and nothing will stand in his way—until he stumbles upon a virgin bride....

Zander took his chances on the streets rather than spending another moment under his cruel father's roof. Now he is unrivaled in business—and the bedroom! He wants the best people around him, and Charlotte is the best PA! Can he tempt her over to the dark side...?

A SHAMEFUL CONSEQUENCE
Available in March

AN INDECENT PROPOSITION
Available in April

HP13053